Toni Morrison's
124 BELOVED

Selected Stories from the 2020
Literary Taxidermy Short Story Competition

Edited by
MARK MALAMUD

124 BELOVED

First Regulus Press printing November 2020
Signal Library 10-0202-13-01

Regulus Press, Seattle WA
www.regulus.press

ISBN: 1736097415
ISBN-13: 978-1-7360974-1-0
(Regulus Press)

OPPORTUNITIES FOR FUTURE TAXIDERMY

"One beast and only one howls in the woods by night. See! sweet and sound she sleeps in granny's bed, between the paws of the tender wolf."
—ANGELA CARTER, "THE COMPANY OF WOLVES"

"The ship didn't have a name. I like long stories."
—IAIN M. BANKS, *CONIDER PHLEBAS*

"Amoebae leave no fossils. Swee-eet!"
—TOM ROBBINS, *EVEN COWGIRLS GET THE BLUES*

"She enters, deliberately, gravely, without affectation, circumspect in her motions (as she's been taught), not stamping too loud, nor dragging her legs after her, but advancing sedately, discreetly, glancing briefly at the empty rumpled bed, the cast-off nightclothes. Perhaps today then … at last!"
—ROBERT COOVER, *SPANKING THE MAID*

"My name is Laura Palmer, and as of just three short minutes ago, I officially turned twelve years old! I have to be numb."
—JENNIFER LYNCH, *SECRET DIARY OF LAURA PALMER*

"A is for Amy who fell down the stairs. Z is for Zillah who drank too much gin."
—EDWARD GOREY, *THE GASHLYCRUMB TINIES*

"The child's world changed late one afternoon, though she didn't know it. In a while she would follow."

—NICOLA GRIFFITH, *HILD*

"This I the first time I've worked without a net. Perhaps we wished there was not so much time."

—THOMAS McGUANE, *PANAMA*

"All this happened, more or less. One bird said to Billy Pilgrim, '*Poo-tee-weet?*'"

—KURT VONNEGUT JR, *SLAUGHTERHOUSE-FIVE*

"Until then, he had never dwelled on the pleasures of memory. These things we know, but not what he felt when he went down into his final darkness."

—JORGE LUIS BORGES, "THE MAKER"

"We went to the Moon to have fun, but the Moon turned out to completely suck. Everything must go."

—M. T. ANDERSON, *FEED*

124 was spiteful.
↓
Beloved.

—Toni Morrison, first and last line from *Beloved*

CONTENTS

Introduction

Welcome to *124 Beloved*, the anthology that collects the ten prize-winning stories from the Toni Morrison contest of the 2020 Literary Taxidermy Short Story Competition.

Literary taxidermy is a story-writing process that involves taking the first and last sentence from a well-known work (often a novel, sometimes a short story) and then "re-stuffing" what goes in-between those lines to create a new, wholly-original work. The goal of the literary taxidermist is not just to slap someone else's words onto the start and finish of an otherwise stand-alone story, but to take full ownership of the borrowed lines, interpreting (or re-interpreting) them in order to make them seamless, integral, and in fact the *perfect* start and finish for a *new* story.

The origin of literary taxidermy is *The Gymnasium*, a collection of nineteen stories written between 2003 and 2017 that "re-stuff" classic works by Milan Kundera, Thomas Wolfe, Ian Fleming, and others. It was a clear example of creative parsimony on the part of the author (some might call it laziness), leveraging the words of other writers to jump-start the creative process. Yet rather than ending up as a pastiche or spoof of other (granted, far better) writers, the stories turned out to be very much their own thing. And it made one wonder: What would happen if rather than having a single writer tackle the first and last lines of a variety of classic works, you had a *variety* of writers tackle the *same* lines? What would that collection be like?

Which brings us to the anthology you hold in your hands and the competition that produced it. The Literary Taxidermy Short Story Competition, sponsored for the third year by Regulus Press, invites writers to stitch together their own stories using the opening and closing sentences of specific works of fiction. For the 2018 competition, participants were given three choices: *The Thin Man* written by Dashiell Hammett; *Through the Looking-Glass* by Lewis Carroll; or "A Telephone Call" by Dorothy Parker. For the 2019 competition, co-edited with Paul Van Zwalenburg, they were given *Fahrenheit 451* by Ray Bradbury.

This year, for the 2020 competition, aspiring writers were given two choices: Aldous Huxley's *Brave New World* and Toni Morrison's *Beloved*.

The present anthology contains stories from the Morrison contest. That means that every story you're about to read starts and ends *exactly* the same way—with the first and last lines of *Beloved*. Of course *the path* that each author takes from beginning to end is unique—and therein lies a particular thrill of reading these short works: despite sharing a common frame, they are all *different*.

So some of the stories in this collection are dark, some are playful, some are surreal, some rhyme, and some are just *strange*. They cross genres; they cross continents (and occasionally planets); and they vary in style and diction and tone and voice. Reading each one is like getting a peek at the results of someone else's Rorschach test.

The authors are eclectic, too. They range in age from twenty-four to sixty-three. They also span the globe, so you're about to read stories from the United States, the United Kingdom, and Australia. (And that's why you may notice stories written in British and American English—so don't be shocked to find *biscuit* in one story and *cookie* in the next.) The winning author in this year's Morrison contest is Erika Bauer, a teacher in Michigan. But she's no newcomer to literary taxidermy: her first published story, "A Dark and Final Space," was included in last year's anthology, *Pleasure to Burn*. This year's story, "You Know, He Knew, I Said," is even better, bending Morrison's lines to tell a complicated story of love, companionship, and grief.

But there's more to these stories than the pleasure found

in their distinction or their differences. Their *similarities* can be just as intriguing.

Yes, you will find a number of tales within this collection focused on resentment—after all, the opening line is *124 was spiteful.*

And the last line—*Beloved*—guarantees there are numerous stories that orbit an object of affection.

But *those* similarities are not particularly interesting. What's interesting are the similarities that appear in story after story that are *unexpected.* For example, this contest received a statistically-improbable number of stories that include apricots, lab experiments, and French kissing. Why? What is it about *those* two lines by Toni Morison that trigger *these* particular narrative neurons to fire?

Literary taxidermy is nothing if not a kind of inkblot test, an invitation to interpret and then riff inside an ambiguous narrative frame. Even if the bizarre similarities that emerge are inexplicable (and really: why *do* so many of the Morrison stories concern apricots?), it shouldn't be a shock that the same input yields similar output. And yet the black box in-between—the human imagination—remains a mystery.

The stories in this anthology were selected by the editors at Regulus Press. The winning story was selected by a panel of eight professional-writer judges. After each story, you'll find a short biographical note about the author, and maybe—just maybe—*you* can figure out how they ended up writing the story they did!

Mark Malamud
5 October 2020

L. F. Falconer

Best Kept Secret

124 WAS SPITEFUL, in a devilish sort of way, with an indelible hint of malice lurking in the corner of his smile. Amanda Drake warmed to the youth immediately and raised her bidding paddle, wondering how, in this day and age, the Rotary Club could continue to call their biggest annual fundraising event a Slave-for-a-Day Auction. But its name was really none of her concern. After all, wasn't she here to secure a strong young man willing to bend the knee, so to speak? It simply was what it was. As swiftly as she had bid, she was outbid. Amanda raised her paddle again, and again. When she finally escorted the young man out of the building at the cost of $800, she considered him a bargain. His name was David.

"I do hope you have your own transportation," Amanda said once out on the street. "It'd be silly of me to call an Uber when you're heading to my house anyway."

"Yeah, I got a car," he said, pointing to a black Dodge Charger halfway down the block. "With the kind of money you just spent on me, I'm surprised you don't."

"I do." Amanda took several steps forward, leaning on her cane. "But I don't drive. Was that your wife who kept trying to outbid me, or simply another admirer?"

"Girlfriend," David answered, donning his sunglasses—inexpensive Wayfarer knock-offs, Amanda noted, but they matched his generic jeans as well.

"I'm sorry I spoiled your plans, David. But today I need you more than she."

"No problem. I could use a break." He paced his gait to match Amanda's labored steps. Upon reaching his car he opened the passenger door.

"It's refreshing to see gallantry is alive and well. Thank you." Clasping her cane, Amanda slid inside.

"I was taught to respect my elders."

"But do you do it out of respect? Or merely because it's expected?"

An Elvis-inspired sneer curled his lip. "Because you recognize the difference, Mrs. Drake, for you it's out of respect."

No matter how the day progressed, she knew he'd suit her purpose and she buckled her seat belt with a smile.

David settled into the driver's seat. "So, what kind of day do I have ahead of me?" he asked while programming Amanda's address into the navigation system.

Amanda stroked the aluminum shaft of her cane and eyed him with just the right amount of daring. "Oh, like your girlfriend, my plans involve a bed." She couldn't see his eyes behind the dark sunglasses, but an apprehensive rise of one brow above the frame accompanied disdain upon his lips.

"I didn't sign up for—"

"Relax, David. You're a little young for my taste. I'm not playing a game of *Fuck, Marry, Murder*. Besides, I've already done all that." She gave him a sly nod. "I just need you to help me clean up the mess."

Again, the well-groomed eyebrow arced and Amanda broke into a full-bodied laugh.

"Such a serious Gus, you are! All I need from you is to finish putting together a planting bed for my kitchen garden. Think you can manage that?"

His relief was audible, and he pulled the Charger into the street. "It's kind of late in the season for a garden, isn't it?"

"At my age, tomorrow is never a promise. You do things

while you can. I don't mind getting my hands dirty now and then. Sometimes I enjoy puttering around the yard a little, and a few days ago, on a whim, I bought what I needed to start a small herb and vegetable garden. I do so enjoy a fresh salad, don't you?"

"Um-hum."

"Andrew—that's my husband—volunteered to build me a raised bed for it, and I thought, How nice! He's actually going to spend the time to make something special for me, like he used to do in our early years. But he cheated. He bought a cheap kit, pre-cut and pre-drilled. All he needed to do was screw it together. But before he did that, he left town and I have dozens of seedlings to plant. So, you see, I need you, David, to help me undo the pickle Andrew left me in."

"Your husband just up and left you?"

Amanda gazed out at the passing scenery. "Not forever. Yet it is what it is, and my seedlings can't wait."

After a long silence, David broke it. "Don't worry, Mrs. Drake. You'll get your garden growing."

Amanda sighed. "Yes. With your help, I will. A garden needs to be tended with love. Without love, it's merely vegetation. Don't you agree?"

"Um, sure."

His lie reassured her, and with a satisfied smile, she relaxed in her seat.

When the navigation system brought him to the wrought iron gates of the fence that surrounded Amanda's estate, David's surprise underscored his question.

"You live here?"

Beyond the gate, at the end of a straight, paved driveway was an apricot-colored Edwardian mansion, completely wrapped on both stories in bright white porches. An expansive lawn lay dappled beneath the shade of old oaks and new maples. Amanda opened the gate with a remote code on her mobile phone. "It's smaller than it looks. A third of the whole damn house is nothing but porches, but it's home. There's a service road ahead on the left, just past that lilac bush. It'll take us around back so we don't have to walk so far."

After pulling into the parking area behind the main house, David killed the engine and scanned the surrounding yard with his signature disdain. Amanda got out of the car and leaned on her cane. "Over this way, son. It really shouldn't take but an hour. The worst of it has already been done."

A long row of tea roses graced the south edge of a white gazebo off the back of the house. Across a short, sunny expanse of lawn near the back porch, bags of topsoil were mounded beside stacks of lumber. A section of freshly tilled earth, level and free of grass, eight feet long and four feet wide, was blocked off between the posts mounted within each corner.

David scanned the unfinished project. "You could've hired someone to build this for a lot cheaper than what you paid for me, you know. Don't you have a gardener?"

"As luck would have it, his wife died several days ago, so Andrew gave him a few weeks off. Besides, the money went to charity, so…."

David continued to scan the prepped area. "It almost looks like a gravesite."

"Well, that's always a possibility now, isn't it?"

Amanda noted the hostility creeping from his lips again and she laughed. "You don't like me much, do you?"

"I don't believe liking you was a requirement."

"You're right. But I believe we're a lot alike, you and I."

The scorn in his smile was laced with amusement.

Amanda elucidated: "Though you lack money, you portray yourself as wealthier than you are, drawing attention to yourself and seeking respect with your style and choice of car, but you hold people in contempt. I seek respect and draw attention to myself with an infirmity"—she patted her cane—"and I, too, find most people contemptible. In a roundabout way, we're kindred spirits. That's why I like you." She pointed to the lumber. "The plan called for a bed two planks in height. The wood's all prepared. Once you get those mounted, you can fill it with the topsoil in the bags. There's a drill and some screws on the table. You do know how to run a drill, don't you?"

"I do." David scratched at his chin and stepped over to the table. He glanced back at the freshly tilled soil. "You didn't kill your husband for his money, did you?" He waved his hand toward the house. "For all this?"

Amanda chuckled and hobbled to the water spigot near the edge of the porch. "The house—the money—it was always mine. But his girlfriend didn't understand that."

A slow twist of his neck brought David's hardened gaze back in her direction, and Amanda smiled sweetly in return. She set her cane aside to attach the water hose to the spigot. "Do you really think I killed my husband and buried him here in the backyard for you to cover up?"

David pointed to the bare garden plot. "There's always that possibility, right?"

"It's an interesting idea. Or maybe," Amanda went on, "it's not Andrew that's buried here. Maybe it's his girlfriend. Or maybe, just maybe, it's simply a patch of ground prepped for a kitchen garden." She smiled once more before she shrugged. "Then again, maybe my husband never left town at all and is buried in the garden. Or maybe he left town with his girlfriend and they chose to vanish from the face of the earth. The possibilities are limitless."

David knelt and began to attach the first side plank to the corner posts. "May I ask where your husband is right now?"

Amanda walked, without a limp, to the line of hybrid tea roses at the gazebo, dragging the water hose with her. As she watered the first rose, a creamy Francis Meilland, the moisture deepened the color of the surrounding mulch, a mixture of the old and the new which she'd sprinkled throughout the rose bed yesterday. "The destination on his ticket was Chicago," she answered. "His flight departed last night, but in all honesty, he could be anywhere by now."

David secured another plank in place.

"However, it is possible," Amanda pinched off a browning leaf from the fragrant Summer Surprise rose, "had I killed him, then he never got on that plane. Yet, if someone were to check, I'd bet they'd find his car at the airport and discover he'd checked in for his flight."

"Did you see him off?"

Amanda moved to the next rose in line, a glowing yellow Winter Sun. "It's quite possible that I purchased his ticket. On his computer. With his credit card. It's quite possible that I drove his car to the long-term parking lot—"

"But you can't drive," David reminded her as he secured another plank.

"Ah." Amanda stepped away from the roses and raised her finger. "I said I don't drive, not that I can't. So, just imagine for a moment, David, that I murdered my cheating husband and buried him in what will become my kitchen garden. Imagine that I then purchased his ticket and packed a small, run-of-the-mill carry-on bag, parked his car in the long-term parking lot, then walked into the airport and checked-in his ticket electronically. Then, perhaps, I went into the ladies room and, because you can't leave your luggage unattended, I took the carry-on with me and once inside a stall, I changed my clothes and then left the airport by a different door, because of cameras, you know. Once back outside, I hopped onto a hotel shuttle. Once at the hotel, I might've walked to a bus stop, then disembarked at a restaurant for an early breakfast before calling for an Uber to take me to the auction—"

"You've really thought this through." David placed another plank.

Amanda moved her water hose to the delicate pink Moonstone rose. "Once or twice in my life. What if instead," Amanda spoke passionately, "Andrew really did fly to Chicago. Perhaps I then sent his girlfriend a message from Andrew's computer and lured her here for a rendezvous. Perhaps, when Andrew returns, he'll never know why she disappeared...or where she went. Yet he'll unknowingly feast upon her with every salad I prepare." Amanda turned and eyed David over her shoulder. His eyes were still hidden behind dark lenses, and he stared back in mute disapproval for a moment before continuing his work. But had it truly been disapproval? Or merely morbid curiosity? She turned back and continued moving the water down the line of roses.

"Don't get me wrong, David. Despite his flaws, I loved my husband, but I will not tolerate betrayal." Amanda glanced toward the sky, taking note of the ominous clouds. "It'll storm before long. With luck it will rain. I find rain refreshing, don't you? It promises new life and washes the bitterness away."

"I'm almost finished." David placed the final plank. "You don't really need that cane, do you?"

"No more than you need your sunglasses. Yet they give you an edge, don't they? An air of mystery, because they hide the truth of your soul. Out in public, my cane also provides me an advantage." Amanda bent to inhale the fragrance of the delectable Peace rose before her. "People show a bit more respect to an older woman with a cane. Without it, I am rather invisible. I don't like being taken for granted."

"You strike me as a woman who knows exactly what she wants and knows how to get it. I don't believe anyone should ever dare take you for granted, Mrs. Drake. Not your husband. Not his girlfriend. Not even your slave for a day."

He set his sunglasses on the table and their eyes met. The intensity lingered with thoughts laid bare. A promise unspoken. Yet still, she needed to hear it.

"Have you ever cheated on your girlfriend, David?"

"Never," he told her. "I wouldn't much respect myself if I did."

"And if she cheated on you?"

He released a long sigh. "In that case, I guess the possibilities might be limitless." He began to pour the first bag of soil into the garden bed.

"You know," Amanda mused, inspecting her brilliant red Mister Lincoln for aphids, "if one had a foreknowledge of a crime and willingly helped cover up that crime, one could possibly be convicted of…what's that term I want? Not an accomplice. Not a co-conspirator. Oh, I remember now—as an accessory after the fact."

David continued to pour topsoil into the bed in silence. When the last crumbs of dirt fell from the bag, he spoke. "I suppose if he did so willingly, one could." He looked over at her. "That is, of course, if a crime had been committed."

"Yes, David." Amanda turned back to her roses. "If a crime were actually committed."

Amanda moved the water hose to the next rose. A new rose. One of three new roses, planted only yesterday, the trio providing a delightful blend of blood red and cream, blushing white, and vivid, velvety scarlet blooms:

One Dark Night.

One Best Kept Secret.

And lastly, one Beloved.

"Best Kept Secret"

L.F. FALCONER is a computer operator living in Nevada, in the United States. She is a collector of stones and old glass and an avid gardener, challenging Mother Nature to constant duels. (Sometimes, she says, Mother Nature even lets her win.) She has written seven novels of dark fiction as well as a collection of short stories. Her work has been published in *Weirdbook Magazine*, the *Shallow Waters Flash Fiction Anthology*, and *From the Yonder: A Collection of Horror from Around the World*.

She says: "I never truly know where my stories are going until they take me there, which makes each one an adventure. The first sentence of this year's Literary Taxidermy Short Story Competition was an invitation I couldn't refuse and once the character of Amanda Drake began to take on a life of her own, the entire story fell into place, leaving me with a devious little smile of satisfaction at the end."

Amis Dee

Submission 129

124 WAS SPITEFUL, and beloved.

•

124 was *spiteful*, down, and *soiled*, across. Lexi bit the end of her pencil. 90 was *decadent*, down, and *deceased*, across. 75 was *rangy* and *rusted*. 62, *putsch* and *puerile*. 58, *cursed* and *cantankerous*. Where had everything gone so wrong? Thirty-five minutes and pretty much everything had gone to hell. She glanced back to the top of the crossword, back to where it had all begun with such promise, where 1 was *beautiful* and *beloved*.

•

124 was spiteful which was a shame. 123 was prideful. 120, the same. "Hullo, 3," said 206. "Move aside," said 67 to a somber 66. Lost key for 111. Package for 44. Here at Cardinal House, numbers adorned both the face and the door. Here at Cardinal House, it had always been the case. It was sadly a colorless decimal place. But one day 7's cat slipped past 7's door, and the cat—on light feet—raced to the end of the floor. 4 happened to open the door at that time, and it was clear this escape was more plan than a crime. And this was the way that 7 met 4, and names were exchanged as never before. This is the way that everything changed, and words replaced numbers, and feelings exchanged. Not just for Pete and Mary, of course, but also their pets—since they were the source—named Love (a tabby) and Beloved (a blue). So for words, neighbors 7 and

4 need only a few. *Pete* and *Mary*, to start, and to follow just two—*Love* and *Beloved*. It's really what counts. And thus Pete and Mary are pleased to announce: from city apartment to heaven above, love and be loved, love and beloved.

•

124 was spiteful, low-cut, and body-hugging—a simple reminder of everything you could never have. A sublime admixture of silk and contempt. Djinna smiled. Such sartorial perfection was rare on the catwalk. "We might sell a few of those," they whispered, and their partner circled the item in her program. "Let's hope, D. Let's hope." 125 was next, a little black number that left little to the imagination. Djinna shook their head. "Too obvious. Over it." "So over," their partner concurred, "so totally *ove*." She struck the item out with a large X. 126 was the color and shape of flame. Djinna's eyes narrowed. As the model moved down the runway, the fiery fabric seemed to lick at her body. "Temptress," Djinna groaned. "Seductress," their partner agreed. "Femme fatale." "Wanton strumpet." "Hot *couture*." "The jezebel look—can't move it." "Won't sell." "So totally *ove*." Their partner returned to the catalog and crossed it out. Djinna looked around. Several people were already standing. Some press, some sponsors, a few celebrities. "Is that it?" they asked. Their partner flipped through the rest of the catalog. No more numbers. Just ads and bios. She sighed, then capped her pen. This was going to be a lean year for *M Alice*, their label. "*Ove*, D."

•

124 was spiteful ok beloved.

•

One twenty for Was. Spiteful, he tossed the Franklin back in Father Oswald's face. "I don't need your charity." Oswald shrugged, didn't bother to pick up the discarded bill. He turned to Haskel, next one in line, and peeled off another twenty. This one was received eagerly; and thus Oswald proceeded down the line of workers, one after another, gifting twenty after twenty until he'd given them all away. All, except the one still on the ground at Was' feet. Yes, Was was still there. He could have left, could have stormed off, but he'd stuck around until the end. "I don't need any charity!" he repeated. "Not from you, not from anyone!" Father Oswald sighed. "You will always be welcome here. You will always be loved."

•

124 was spiteful, but you couldn't say he was stupid. Emily had run nearly 300 rats through the maze, but this one—number 124—was the only one to master it. Yet he showed contempt for his human captor, and even the carrot treat offered as a reward at the end of a session was often met with a snarly bite. *Well, two can play that game,* Emily thought, and on Thursday, black Sharpie in hand, she wagged a finger at the rodent, grinned, crossed out his number and gave him a name: *Beloved.*

•

One 24 was spiteful; the other, skillful. You could see it easily the first time you saw either on the football pitch. One kicked at shins to make a point; the other dribbled and outwitted. One complained when the other team scored; the other ran back to the center line and urged his teammates on. Identical numbers on different teams. One was tolerated; the other, beloved.

•

1:24 was spiteful. *And the spies saw a man come forth out of the city, and they said unto him, Shew us, we pray thee, the entrance into the city, and we will shew thee mercy.* But there was no city. The biblical passage was a trick. A trap. But why? Something in our stars? Something in ourselves? Something in our blood? Something in our cells? Simon pleaded before the judge, but the judge was unmoved. Neither one, in the end, was beloved.

•

124 was *Spite*, full of bitter soda that, if you dared to taste, would make your face pucker up and look like that cartoon prostitute on the candy roll right next to it, 147, *StreeTarts*. "A fishy taste for a fishy product," or so its grimy wrapper proclaimed. Next to 147 was 12, *Milky Whey*. "Comes in your mouth, not in your hands." Heh-heh. Some nights Tommy would sit at the foot of his bed and stare at his collection of nearly forty life-sized parody products, collected over years and years (or at least during most of fifth grade). He hadn't opened any of them, of course. That would obliterate their value as collector's items. In fact, he rarely even took them off the shelf. Except for one, which he was drawn towards like no other. The prize of his collection, catalog number 201, smack dab in the center of his display—under the shelf with his baseball mitt and baseball cards, and above the shelf with his collection of Rubber-Man comic books—a mint-condition still-in-the-box squeeze tube of *Johnson & Johnson's Heart Remover*. Its tagline: "Not everyone needs to be loved."

•

124 was spiteful. 125 had terrible spelling. 126 was hackneyed. 127 was incomprehensible. Submission 128 was racist *and* sexist. And 129 was all over the place, yet somehow beloved.

"Submission 129"

AMIS DEE is a GIS developer living in Arizona, in the United States. She's thirty-two years old, but is proud of her lengthy résumé which includes time as a software editor, a graphics designer, an awkward ballerina, an animator, and a singer in an all-girl karaoke band. She has been published online, but "Submission 129" is her first published short story.

She says: "I didn't know what to do with the Morrison lines. Nothing seemed to stick. I kept starting and giving up. But after a few beers with some friends, I decided why limit myself to just one story? Why not just do them all?"

Khariya Ali

A Songbird's Silence

124 WAS SPITEFUL. Today even more so than usually.

123 reeks of cheap liquor and stale cigarette smoke, but is a little bored of his task. When he raises his fists, it always seems a bit lacklustre. Poor man can't put his heart into it, and it shows. There are things he'd rather be doing; places he'd rather be. He doesn't have the morality to be repulsed by his task—they drill that out before sending them in—but he has done it for long enough it's nothing of note to him.

125 is newer, you can just tell. In another life he'd have made a fine civil servant. He never pulls punches, but they aren't spiteful. They are clean, efficient, professional. For him it's about a job well done. He could just as diligently wear a suit and file paperwork as break jaws.

124, though, is spiteful. He's the one who will tweak a broken nose, or aim an extra kick at the shins. He'll pull hair and twist it, unable to keep that little bit of a smile off his face as he does. When he comes into the cell, you can tell there's nothing else he'd rather be doing. It isn't a job for him, it's a godsend—an opportunity for a sadist to indulge himself every day and be paid for it to boot.

124 smiled when he broke my ribs, and as the others leave the cell he presses his boot just hard enough to hurt, putting one foot atop my crumpled body like a new land he's claiming for King and Country. I look in his eyes and see a slathering hunger to go further. But he has orders—pain is the name of the game; death isn't. So, he lifts his foot eventually, and walks out, letting the cell door slam shut behind him.

The guards don't show inmates their names. They don't even call each other by them in front of us. All an act—ostensibly for security, but who the hell would any of us tell? No, it's about control. They can't make the men who beat us faceless, so they just make them nameless. The King's men are numbers, and we are names. It seems a strange twist of fate that prisoners should have more individuality than their captors—but that is the point, I suppose. It is who we are that landed us here, and it is who we are that they punish. If we had been nameless, kept our heads down, maybe we could be the ones with our boot pressing down into someone else's chest.

So I memorise their numbers. They are stitched onto their uniforms—at the front and on the arm. The 1 on 124's uniform is fraying—the bottom stitches are coming loose. I know that because he likes to get close to my face when he applies the hot irons. Sometimes he whispers in my ear that if I just cry, he'll stop.

When I get out of this place, he'll be the first one I kill—and I'll do it slowly.

There's the sound of a bell ringing faintly in the distance. I hear it chime; once, twice. Lunch time. Interrogation will be over for the morning.

It takes some of the newer prisoners a while to realise it isn't really about information. They go in stubborn as mules, with secrets to protect and noble ideas about courage and justice and honour. They will be martyrs, they think, for the great and noble cause. They will be the stuff of legends and songs and history books.

If the only purpose of all of this was to take our lives, maybe they would be right. But we don't die here—not until we've slipped out of memory, and out of the potential of redemption. Not until we've yielded our secrets and begged for death over and over and over. Not until we've betrayed our friends, and our beliefs, and we no longer believe in any salvation.

The medics will be here soon, ready to pull inmates from cells and patch them back together, just well enough to be pretty sure they won't die. Then back to the interrogation tomorrow.

They've stopped even asking me questions. I'm glad—we've dropped pretence. They want to see us defeated, humiliated, broken. Every blow, every burn, every cut: "this is what happens when you step out of place." Our crime isn't really trying to kill the King—it's daring to want to. There are grand men who have ordered the world just so, we presumed to challenge their authority, their decisions, so they take our choices, and leave us only their control.

The door opens with a groan.

"Morrison!" It's 124 again, now accompanied by the medic—a twitchy little man I've not seen before. "Why don't you tell Doc where it hurts so he can make it all better?"

Bastard. No doubt my gaze burns with hatred as I struggle up into a sitting position, collapsing against a wall and panting from exertion. I flash him a smile though, showing bloody teeth.

The medic stumbles back a little, alarmed by my expression. 124 laughs and claps him on the shoulder. "Don't worry, Doc, just our little joke there. This songbird, she ain't been singing in a long time." He chuckles to himself at his own supposed cleverness. Moron.

The medic stares at him blankly.

"God, man!" 124 exclaims. "You must be green—you never heard of Wren Morrison?"

The medic's eyes finally light with understanding. A vainer me from a past life might have been offended that he didn't recognize me. But I can't very well hold that against him—I don't exactly look my best. He's seen the videos, and the posters—of course he has. I watch him take in my emaciated form, and disfigured face. I can see the mental calculation as he tries to work out where the Songbird of the

Revolution is hiding in this wasted, walking corpse. Then he remembers what they did to me—he probably saw that, too. After all, it was televised.

"Don't worry, Doc." 124 continues, smiling at me maliciously. "She's no danger to anyone anymore." He pushes past the medic and sits himself down on the bed in my cell, crossing his legs and leaning back.

One day I will prove him wrong.

The medic shuffles over timidly, but stops short of me and looks nervously to 124, a question clearly on his mind.

"Hurry it up, Doc," 124 groans. "We've got more to see after this." He strides over to where I sit and pulls me up by my hair. My hands go up instinctively and I claw at his knuckles impotently to try to ease the grip that drags me up. My ribs protest, vociferously. "Just broken ribs and a few burns," he tells the medic. "Set them, bandage them, and we can go." He tosses me like a ragdoll onto the bed where an animal groan escapes my lips.

The medic pales, but he sets about his work. His hands flutter with apprehension as he puts them to my injuries, but I can't fault his handiwork. His eyes avoid my face—I prefer that over the grim fascination some of his predecessors have watched me with. It hurts when he sets my ribs—three were broken—but he does it fast and deftly.

My mind wanders as he works—it often does. There is nothing in my world anymore to keep my mind from wandering—and I would not wish to stop it, the paths it walks are much more pleasant than those of reality. I don't know how long I've spent here. I have no way of counting the days. Others in solitary confinement, it is said, talk to themselves. I have heard of people who produced their *magnum opus* inside prison walls, but I am forbidden pen or paper. I can only think to myself.

Perhaps it will make me mad—at the very least my mind teeters on the knife edge of sanity. I cannot speak, and I cannot even write, so there is nowhere for all the words inside of me to go. They beat furiously at the walls of my brain, desperate to be heard—caged birds with frantic wings.

The King took my voice with his own hands, and now his prison guards work to make my mind follow suit. My thoughts are always clamouring over one another—they trip and stumble and crowd for space and attention—sometimes I think my head will split. I am stitched together by the medics, but the only thread holding the shredded fragments of my sanity together is *vengeance*.

Is that ignoble?

Once, my values would have told me to say *hope*. I believed in hope. I sung about hope before, and those songs inspired men and women to fight. But they killed hope a long time ago. They left ashes where we hoped to plant new seeds. Now I hold on for the chance to make ashes of men like 124.

"Is that too tight?" the medic asks as he fastens the last bandage, directing the question to 124. People do that often—like when they cut out my tongue, I turned deaf.

124 shrugs. "Who cares? Not like she's about to complain—are you Morrison?"

I bristle, but I say nothing.

The medic gathers his bag and walks to the door. 124 remembers my food as he walks out—it is on the cart with everyone else's. He grins at me as he places the bowl of gruel on the floor where he knows I will have to bend to get it.

Like I said, spiteful.

The door closes, but I know he will be watching me on the live camera feed as I struggle across the cell to pick up the paltry meal. My eyes flicker up to its unblinking red light, nestled into the smooth surface of the wall, ever watchful.

There are no windows to my cell. There is only the door. All the walls are smooth concrete—no purchase for fingers to find. The bed is concrete too, with a single sheet for warmth. Toilet breaks are twice a day—the guards enter to watch when the foul-smelling latrine emerges briefly from the wall. Occasionally I am allowed to wash, carried blindfolded to a communal shower that runs either scorching hot or freezing cold, and doused with soap to prevent lice.

When they come for interrogations, they bring chairs—so they can make us sit. But they take them with them when they leave.

The bowl my food is served in is plastic, there is no cutlery.

The lights run the length of the ceiling, and are flush with concrete so there is nothing to grab—too high anyway to be reached. Sometimes they leave them on at night—I suspect that's also 124.

I slide down the edge of the bed onto the floor, pausing for a breath before shuffling across to the bowl. The movement hurts, but I am too hungry not to make the journey. I sit and sip at the bowl of tasteless watery sludge. Of course, being without a tongue means most things are tasteless. They feed me here to keep me alive, but not enough to keep me strong. And it tasted like shit even when I did have a tongue.

The bowl cleared, I struggle back to the bed, where I lie down and stare at the concrete. Its smooth, unbroken surface should offer a blank canvas to the imagination. I would like to look at it and dream of blue skies and starry nights, but instead its smoothness discomforts me, and my eyes rove it constantly for non-existent fault lines, flaws and fissures.

I know this cell—how many paces from wall to wall, how many handspans across the bed, how many finger-widths the door is made up of. This is my world—tiny as it is, and my body is trapped here as my words are trapped in my head. My words, though, still put the futile fight against their prison walls; my body has long since realized the pointlessness of that.

When they first brought me here, I shouted and screamed and beat the walls. I tried to strangle guards with my sheet, I raked them with my nails and bit and spat. I sang, and I heard the inmates across the prison clamour in response.

Then the King cut out my song, and silence is all that reigns here now.

God, my ribs hurt. The bandages are too tight. They press too hard and the pressure makes it hard to breathe—especially as I lie down. My fingers move to the knot the medic tied, to try to loosen it. My hands are clumsier than they once were. The knot was tied too well and it takes me time to coax it free. I hate that I fumble now, lacking the dexterity that once came so easily.

The cloth slips free and I let it loosen and give a little, my breathing easing as the pressure subsides, but as I adjust the wrappings, my finger catches on something that doesn't feel right. My thumb brushes it again and I freeze. It feels like paper. Is it a hallucination? Have I finally lost the last vestiges of my sanity?

I pull my sheet up a little, and shift, angling my body towards the wall and away from the camera.

It *is* paper, a small piece lodged in the folds of the bandage that I work loose very gently. Curiosity near overwhelms me. Was it an accident? Why is it there? The questions come in a flurry, fast and fluttering. Gingerly, half-unsure, I unfold the paper and—holding it in my cupped hand out of sight of the ever-watchful eye—I read it.

My heart races, my hands tremble. But I smile.

There are four words written on the scrap of paper.

We are coming, Beloved.

"A Songbird's Silence"

KHARIYA ALI is a paralegal living in London, in the UK. "A Songbird's Silence" is her first published short story.

She says: "The title was the last part of this story to be written. The rest was the occupation of a bright afternoon in May, and the copious free time afforded by lockdown. I've always been fascinated by the written word as an immersive experience; its ability to carry you away and draw you in, leaving you wanting more by the time it releases you. I was able to enjoy a small piece of that while Wren and her world coalesced on paper, and I can only hope that there is equal enjoyment for you in reading it."

Michael R Goodwin

The Wiseman Bridge

124 WAS SPITEFUL.

His real name was Daniel Blau, but he insisted that everyone call him 124. He had the number tattooed on his arm, and said he got it at Auschwitz. None of us questioned him on what he wanted to be called or even where he got the tattoo. There were five of us who lived under the Wiseman Bridge; we all had reasons why we were there, and we all used nicknames instead of the ones we were born with. None of us were in the position to be judgmental.

After 124 had been with us for a few days, I remember thinking that something must have gone terribly wrong in his life for someone like him to wind up under the bridge with the rest of us. He was a smooth talker, charismatic with a kind of confidence that made everything he did seem effortless. He seemed like the kind of guy who would have had it all. His disarming persona earned him a spot with us under the bridge, even though most weren't fond of newcomers.

As I said, he was spiteful, but only when he was being protective of his things. Most of us were a bit possessive as well, being those who had very little by way of earthly possessions at this juncture of our lives. The difference with 124 was that he'd become violent when anyone touched his things. To avoid his mean streak, we all learned to give him a wide berth.

Well, most of us did.

124 always had a cigarette between his lips, but he never

smoked it. Sometimes, late at night, he'd take a beaten-up brass Zippo out of his pocket, flick it open, and stare into the flame. He would hold it just out of reach of the cigarette. Two weeks passed, and he performed this ritual every night. Not once did I see him light his cigarette.

Curiosity got the better of me one night, so I asked him.

"How come you never light it?"

124 jumped, my question startling him. He spun around and in the moonlight I saw something change in his eyes. His pupils were hugely dilated, but they quickly shrunk down to normal size. He smiled.

"Trying to quit, I suppose," he said.

"I've never seen you smoke," I replied.

"That's the thing, Clifford. It doesn't matter what your vice is. Once an addict, always an addict."

He had a point. A lot of us were down here because of a vice. For me, it was alcohol, and like a lot of other alcoholics I knew, I professed that it wasn't my fault that I wound up under the Wiseman Bridge. The things I saw at war came first, and the alcohol came second. Putting the bottle before the family I came home to was third. Whatever path led to the Wiseman Bridge, it was a destination that equalized us all.

"Seems to me like it'd be easier to quit smoking if you didn't always have a cigarette in your mouth and a lighter in your pocket," I countered.

"Some habits are harder to break," 124 said with a shrug. He held up his Zippo and waggled it in the air. "Besides that, Beloved here has seen me through a lot. I just can't seem to part with her."

"Beloved?" I asked.

He nodded. "Mm-hmm. That's what I call her."

The lighter looked similar to one that I was issued in the Army, back before I saw the things that changed me. 124 placed it between his index finger and thumb and spun it around, the moonlight glinting off the sides.

"Not sure what makes it so special," I said. "Looks like one I used to have."

124 laughed. "Yours was not like this, I guarantee it."

"What makes it so special, then?"

While he considered my question, 124 stuck his cigarette behind his ear and stood up. I thought at first that he was going to walk away, but instead he flipped the lighter open. He thumbed the flint and the wick sprang into flame. He carried it over to me, cupping his hand around the flame so the wind wouldn't snuff it out.

"Look at it," he said reverently.

I looked at his face, wondering if he was serious. It was hard to tell, darkness now obscuring his face, but I decided to indulge him.

"What am I looking for?"

"Just hush, you'll see," 124 said.

He brought the lighter closer to me and I stared at it, watching the flame dance from side to side on the wick. Some time passed, and I was about to tell 124 that I was done with his little game when I saw her.

A woman stepped out from behind the flame like it was a curtain. She was more beautiful than any woman I had ever seen in my life. She was made of fire, her hair flowing upward as it glowed red, orange, and yellow. Her eyes were white hot coals, hips swaying seductively as she consumed the air around us. The woman, this stunning Phoenix, grew larger.

I was afraid at first, which soon mixed with an overwhelming feeling of completeness. I was wholly sustained, having no need for anything. The hunger in my stomach was gone. The itch in my brain that only a stiff whiskey could soothe fell quiet. I felt like a dry riverbed receiving water after a drought.

The woman in flames, now standing nearly a foot tall,

extended her hand towards me. Her lips moved, but instead of hearing words I saw images in my mind. I was simultaneously terrified and entranced by her and by what I saw in my mind, and was frozen in place. I felt the heat radiating from her as she leaned down to touch my face.

124 snapped the Zippo closed, and the Phoenix disappeared.

I began to protest, but 124 placed his hand on my shoulder. His grip was strong and caught me off balance. I fell onto my back and he pinned me down, his knee digging painfully into my gut.

"What did you see?" he demanded.

I closed my eyes, replaying what the Phoenix had shown me. I tried to speak, but I found there was no air in my lungs. They felt dry and burnt. I gasped, and the cool night air filled me.

"I saw the sky on fire," I said at last.

He released his grip on my shoulder and stood up, seeming relieved.

"Did you recognize anything? Anyone?"

I shook my head.

Silence fell between us, and for a few minutes the only sounds were of the Androscoggin River babbling and the idle chatter coming from around a barrel fire nearby. The other Wisemen were huddled around it for warmth in a painful display of our stereotype.

"Who is she?" I asked.

"She's my Beloved," 124 answered simply. "She gives me everything I need."

I nodded because I understood. She made me feel the same way when I looked into her flames, but there was something 124 wasn't saying.

"What does she ask for in return?"

124 didn't offer an explanation, as he knew I didn't need one. I already knew what she wanted, because I had seen it

in my head when she spoke to me.

He got up and returned to his spot under the bridge. I returned to mine, all at once exhausted and my mind filled with roiling flames. I unrolled my sleeping bag and crawled in, falling asleep almost immediately.

I woke up to the sounds of shouting and a scuffle.

The sun was rising and the clouds were low, making the sky look like it was on fire. I shivered as a wave of *déjà vu* passed through me. The sky looked exactly as it had in my head the night before, when the Phoenix spoke to me.

"Give it back!" 124 yelled.

He was on the ground, wrestling with the Wiseman that we called Lincoln, so named for his tall stature and penchant for honesty. Lincoln had something clutched in his fist, and was trying to prevent 124 from prying it out.

"It's mine, I found it!" Lincoln cried.

"No, you stole it!"

Lincoln was even less likely to steal than he was to lie (and he never lied), so it was odd to me how he came to possess whatever 124 claimed was his. They fought with each other while the rest of the Wisemen, myself included, gathered round. We didn't intervene; no one ever did when fights broke out. I leaned in close, trying to see what Lincoln had in his hand. Just then, 124 got one of his fingers hooked inside Lincoln's fist and yanked. His fist sprung open and a small metal object went flying: 124's brass Zippo. I shot out my hand and caught it.

124 watched it fly into my hand and scrambled away from Lincoln towards me. He came up and demanded his lighter back as Lincoln, rubbing at a trickle of blood coming from his nose, retreated to his camp.

The Zippo felt comfortable in my hand, like it had belonged to me my entire life. The way I felt when the Phoenix looked at me, that feeling of wholeness, slowly crept back in. I opened my mouth to refuse giving it back, but 124 spoke before I could get the words out.

"She's *mine*," he said coldly.

At that point in my life, I had lived under the Wiseman Bridge for longer than I had been away at war. During my time at war, I learned how to read a man's eyes. It was a survival technique, a tool in my belt that my time under the Wiseman Bridge honed until it was razor sharp. There's a certain look that a man gets in his eyes when he realizes that he's got nothing left to lose...or nothing left to live for. If it hadn't been for what I saw in 124's eyes in that moment, I wouldn't have given the lighter back.

"I know she's yours," I said, scared of what 124 would do if I refused. "I wasn't going to keep her."

I held the lighter out in my palm, and 124 snatched it away. He shoved it deep into the front pocket of his tattered pants and stalked off.

He disappeared for the rest of the day, coming back just as dusk was settling in. I couldn't help but observe him from a distance, trying to ignore the jealousy I felt at seeing the lighter in his hands instead of mine.

As I had seen him do many times, 124 plucked the cigarette from its perch behind his ear and put it in his mouth. He flicked open the lighter and held the flame out to the cigarette. I expected him to hold it out and stare into the flame like he normally did. Instead, he brought the flame under the cigarette and inhaled deeply.

"Finally give in?" I asked. "Decided you needed a smoke?"

He turned to look at me. His eyes were dead, distant.

"No, she did."

"Who did?"

"Beloved."

His behavior was unsettling, so I turned to walk away. 124 grabbed my wrist and pulled me back.

"Beloved gets hungry every now and then," he said, his speech stilted and disjointed. "That's the thing about her, and with all fire, really. Once you start to feed her, once she gets reminded of how good it feels to burn—well, she's fire. She's always going to want more. She's going to burn everything until there's nothing left."

His words chilled me. I knew them to be true because of the other things I saw in my mind when the Phoenix had spoken to me. That spiteful streak, that wild spitefulness we all feared was coming. I tried to backpedal away, yanking my arm down to slip out of his grasp.

124 walked away, a trail of cigarette smoke encircling his head like a crown. I took a few steps back, my heart pounding in my ears.

He pulled out a glass bottle from his pocket as he approached Lincoln's camp. He opened it and poured half onto Lincoln, who was asleep under a blanket. He then took a swig, spilling most of what was left down the front of his jacket in the process.

The distance between 124 and I seemed to grow as I ran towards him. I shouted at him to stop, but when I saw the Phoenix appear in 124's hands I knew it was too late. 124 flicked the cigarette onto Lincoln's blanket, the tip glowing cherry red, and the blanket erupted in flames.

The sound of Lincoln screaming echoed up the Androscoggin. He tried rolling to extinguish the flames, but only succeeded in tangling himself up. The fire around him grew as other objects caught on. The acrid smell of burning flesh filled the air. Lincoln stopped screaming as fire blessedly overcame him.

124 turned to me, the Phoenix dancing in his hands.

"He shouldn't have taken my Beloved," he said.

124 looked like he was going to say something else, but the Phoenix, his Beloved, reached out with her fiery hands and grabbed onto his jacket. Flames licked eagerly at the alcohol that he had spilled on himself and fire spread over him instantly with a percussive rush.

The heat kept me back, but there was nothing that could

be done anyways. I held my jacket over my face as black smoke poured up into the night sky.

124 made no sound as he burned. After a few minutes he dropped to his knees, and then fell over on top of Lincoln. The Phoenix consumed them both.

Doc and Simon, the other Wisemen, rushed in with blankets to smother the flames to no avail. When the inferno eventually died down, Doc rolled Lincoln and 124 over to see if by any chance either of them were still alive. They weren't.

The Zippo fell out of 124's hands when they rolled him over. It bounced off the gravel and landed at my feet. I picked it up, expecting it to be hot to the touch. Instead it was quite cool.

I turned and walked back towards my camp. I opened the Zippo and flicked the flint wheel. The Phoenix stepped out of the flame and spoke to me.

She was mine now, she said.

Mine.

Beloved.

"The Wiseman Bridge"

MICHAEL R GOODWIN is a tax and regulatory specialist living in Maine, in the United States. In addition to writing fiction, he enjoys photography and composing music. He prefers to write in the dark while listening to classical music (usually Mozart's Requiem in D Minor). "The Wiseman Bridge" is his first published short story.

He says: "Inspiration for this story came from the definition of the word spiteful: 'showing or caused by malice.' It made me consider what would drive someone to allow themselves to be overcome, even temporarily, by a desire for evil. With that in mind, I wrote this story in one go, sitting at my kitchen table with a glass of whiskey."

Julia Jordan

The Salvation of 1-2-4

1-2-4 was spiteful
She snarled and swiped and hissed
She scratched me as I picked her up
This cat will not be missed

Other cats who had been lost
Were waiting to be found
It was a normal afternoon
Of life here at the pound

We walked past all the cages
Of cats still in their prime
Unfortunately for 1-2-4
She'd now run out of time

We took a right past 1-0-1
A sweet and mellow cat
I looked at 1-2-4 and said
"You should have been like that!"

I took her down a hallway
To her impending doom
Left then right then left again
To the injecting room

But then the sound of little feet
And giggling did I hear
As 1-2-4 re-scratches me
A boy and girl appear

"Can we see that cat?" they said
"We'd love one just like her"
And to my shock I heard a sound:
1-2-4 began to purr!

That cat jumps from my arms to theirs
They pat her in delight
I hope she will not scratch them
No; she plays with all her might!

The kids and cat were boisterous
I was pushed around in jest
I pondered as I stumbled back
"These kids bring out her best!"

I thought again and smiled now
As I was once more shoved
1-2-4's not spiteful
She just needed to be loved

"The Salvation of 1-2-4"

JULIA JORDAN is a part-time non-profit grant writer living in Melbourne, Australia. Although trained as a lawyer, she now spends most of her time raising two small children. Her favorite things include sunshine, porch swings, baked goods, and her family. "The Salvation of 1-2-4" is her first published work.

She says: "I have a two-year-old and a four-year-old, and my days are filled with picture books and toddler songs—so it is not surprising that my literary taxidermy features animals and rhyming verse! The idea came to me on a sleepless night, and the poem was tweaked over many subsequent nights as my mind travelled through the alphabet trying to find the right words to rhyme together."

You Know, He Knew, I Said

124 WAS SPITEFUL. Tracing the route of modern I-40, NM 124 kicked dirt and nostalgia into the face of the interstate. It was open and worn and reckless, like an artifact, daring us to touch it, to feel the heartbeat of Route 66 thunder up through the tires, pulsate through the steering wheel and into the cabin—oxygen that was dirty and pure. Driving through McCartys, New Mexico, the wheel of the Chevy Chevelle loosely gripped in his left hand, James looks out at the horizon, once again seemingly bewitched by the Zuni Mountains, just west of our destination in Grants, fixated by the lava flow, the *malpais*, all around us. Out of the corner of my eye I watch him roll down his window and put his hand flat against the wind. I know the sensation: all that nothing that feels like something right in the palm of your hand.

Leaning against the passenger window, I watch as 124 curves to the south. I try to read James' eyes but it's hard. The late afternoon sun is ruthless and his profile is unrelenting. We haven't spoken much since Tucumcari, both of us sober and entranced by waves of heat melting the road ahead, an urban mirage made more magical by a terrain so vastly open. And though we haven't spoken and it's quiet, except for the hum of the Chevelle, it's not a quiet that waits for words to fill it. Me and James, we finish each other's silences.

That's how I know that James needs a drink—because I need a drink—a little something to smooth the rough places beneath the surface of his jaw. We have a gig later that night

53

in Flagstaff, but that's still hours off.

First, there's Grants.

I reach over and put my hand on the back of James' neck. Today is an anniversary, the only one he celebrates, and I know that the closer we get to Grants, the more his hands will betray him, the more the muscles in his jaw will twitch, some mystery of biology that only men learn how to do. So even though I've heard the story before, I ask him to tell it to me again.

"Tell me how you met, that night out in the desert. Pretty, the way you always do," I ask. I roll down my window and light a cigarette, inhale slowly while he thinks about it. I pass it to him, lipstick-stained and ready, the way we both like it.

James takes a long drag and the road becomes a slight hill and the sun falls imperceptibly lower in the sky. He looks at me with a silent question, looking for the place to start. I run my hand through his hair, slowly, waiting, until he finds the way.

"I was coming home after playing a late set in Albuquerque," he says. "One of those dark bars named after a woman, full of men. You know the type, Layla. Our kind of place." He laughs and I lean my head back against the seat, picturing the bar and James and the darkness. "You weren't there that night. You were back at that shitty motel, sick. So I played that night alone. It was strange from the beginning, you know?"

"Yeah, I remember," I say, not because he's really asking, but because this is his story, and his story has a rhythm. I look toward the mountains, expansiveness and isolation all around us, James' voice like a map to an unmarked road.

"After the set, I'm packing up my gear and these guys offer to buy me a round. They introduce themselves. Tough guys, Layla. You know, like South Side Chicago meets John Wayne, if you can believe it. But I'm thirsty and it's late, so

I let 'em." I picture James that night—dark jeans, black boots, short thick hair standing up in rebellion. Stubble on his face. That scar about his left eye that you never forget.

"So we're drinking, me and these guys, and I notice him for the first time—Mick. He's sitting around the L of the bar—shorter build, all shoulders and chin, something in his eyes that tells you there's probably a box of shells in his glove compartment. And he's looking at me. Looking at me in that way when you know someone's doing everything not to look at you. And he's got this blond on his arm, and she's holding on to him just so as not to fall shitfaced on the floor. And Layla," James pauses here, like he always does, because he doesn't have the words. No matter how many times he tells it, he doesn't have the words. "When he looked at me, I couldn't fucking breathe. I'm holding this whiskey and laughing at some shit the guy next to me is saying, and he looks at me, and all of a sudden I can't breathe."

And I can see it, James and Mick—James like some cowboy who stumbled into a Calvin Klein ad, those lanky muscled arms, that quiet indifference; Mick like a young Jack Dempsey, a face made more handsome by bruises and scars, that reckless punch.

"So it's getting late, and the guys are leaving, and I got nowhere to be, so I order another shot. The guys pat me on the back, tell me to come around next time I'm in town, make a couple jokes about all the shit they're gonna take when they get home to their girls. And Mick and the girl he's with, she's putting on her sweater, and he walks up to me to shake my hand, and he says, 'Take it easy, man.' And I grab his hand, Layla, and my heart is pounding so loud I swear you can hear the bass. And you know I'm not shy, so when I shake his hand, I really touch his hand and I say, 'You too,' and the sleeve of my jacket brushes his chest when I turn. Like I could feel it."

James stops for a second because he's said a lot, said it in a way he wouldn't normally say out loud. But then he sees me. It's just me. And he goes on, the sun over 124 just beginning to haze as we head past Anzac.

"He walks out the door, arm around the blond, and I watch him go, like that—me, just nursing that last double whiskey. After a while it gets quiet, and you know how I hate last call, so I head out. I walk to the Chevelle, inhaling that desert air and the cigarette in my hand. I stop in front of my door, just looking at my reflection in the glass, smoking, when I see this shadow over my shoulder. And as I'm getting ready to turn around, his puts his hand on my shoulder, like he owns it, and he says, 'So…where we going?' I turn around and I don't say anything and it's so fucking loud in my head and he says, 'I had to get rid of them. You know…the guys, the girl. Took a few minutes.' And there's this long moment where I'm looking at him, just looking, and then I reach for the back of his neck and he hesitates, flinches for a second, looks around him like a criminal, and when he looks back, I see it. It's like his eyes jump forward. And he grabs me the second before I grab him, and I kissed him in the parking lot, kissed him like we were fighting, cigarette still in hand, kissed him the way you claw yourself back to sleep when you're getting to the good part. When you don't want to wake up."

James reaches for the cigarette again and I can't tell if the story's over because I know all the endings. I know how James drove Mick back to our motel that night, how I could hear them through the paper walls of the motel room—laughing and loud, quiet and pretend-motionless. I know how James dropped him back off at his car the next morning, the way the sun glinted off the windshield as they said goodbye, how every time James played at the bars, there'd be this song that I know he played for Mick, wherever he was. I know how they saw each other that year whenever we drove through New Mexico, how James, who was always bold, always what he was, wanted to hold him in broad daylight. And how Mick, no matter how beautiful James was, would only say it when they were alone.

The blankness of Route 66 gives way as we enter Grants.

We pass the Junkyard Brewery and head into Downtown—
a right on 1st avenue, another right on Roosevelt. Five
minutes tops and we'd be there. I wait a bit before asking
the question because it doesn't feel right to talk about Mick
while there's a fucking AutoZone or Pizza Hut in the
backdrop. But we're almost there and so I ask him right
before we turn onto 1st, while the mountains are still to our
left, while there's still something beautiful to look at.

"Are you ready to see him?"

James looks in the rearview mirror, runs his hand
through his hair. "Yeah," he says. "I'm ready." And then,
"You can come too."

"Always," I say.

We turn onto Roosevelt and ease into the parking lot.
James gets out of the car. By now it's closing in on the final
breaths of sun, daylight burning like whiskey—slow and
steady. I follow James to the meeting spot, always close
behind until we see Mick. I find a big oak tree a couple
dozen paces behind James and sit down, pull another
cigarette from my jeans.

James walks up to the spot and I look out at the trees, so
green after so many mountains. "Sorry I'm late," he says,
and sits down on the grass. He puts his hand against the
gravestone, and then his forehead, and I don't need to look
to know that he's whispering. I don't need to listen to know
what he says. He doesn't cry because it isn't him, but he
holds his chest tight and the muscles of his forearms are
stiff. Someone passing by might think he's trying to rip a
chunk of concrete from the top of the slab, his fingers more
than just holding on in the dipping sunlight.

From beneath the tree, I can see portions of the
headstone, "Michael," "1977," "Beloved son and brother."
I watch as James traces the name with his finger. When he
comes to the word "Beloved," he hesitates, his whole body
caught in the inhale. I know James, so I know he's thinking
about the funeral, his place in the back, how no one there

knew who he was, how he couldn't tell them because Mick didn't tell them.

Time, no matter what anyone says, is irrelevant. How long or how short. Love takes nothing. But I don't say this to James. He lets me sit here because I don't say obvious shit to him, or tell him it's going to be ok, or promise him that this too will pass. I watch him touch the word again and stand up in front of Mick's grave.

"Such a bullshit word, you know?" he says. "A word you hear at fucking weddings and gravesites. No one says it in real life. It feels strange to say it in real life. *Beloved.*" He says it like a curse.

I walk up behind him, lean against his back, pull the collar of his shirt down, and kiss the back of his neck lightly. I keep leaning against him, letting the word wash over me, too. Whispered. Archaic. Made only for stone. And before I nudge his elbow, telling him it's time to go, I lean in closer.

"You know, he knew," I say. "Even if you never said it."

And James, like 124, like always, walks away—with me.

"Come on, Layla."

We head back to the Chevelle—James in front, me a step behind. I watch James' silhouette move against the New Mexican horizon as the sun sets, wondering where we'll sleep tonight, wondering if we'll sleep tonight.

Back on Route 66, Grants a few miles behind us, I look toward the darkening skies of Black Rock ahead. James rolls down his window and inhales the night like it's more than oxygen. I pass him a cigarette so he can breathe. Dusk rolls in like there's no need for another sunrise.

I wonder how the darkness can be this soft.

James thinks of Mick. I think of James. The fading, open road thinks of nothing. And everything aches to say what cannot be said: looking ahead, lost behind, words be damned.

Beloved.

"You Know, He Knew, I Said"

ERIKA BAUER is a teacher in Michigan, in the United States. Stephen King was the soundtrack of her childhood, and her first short story as a teenager was inspired by Anne Rice. Her first published story, "A Dark and Final Space," was a finalist in last year's Literary Taxidermy anthology, *Pleasure to Burn*, and this year's story is even better: we loved its sad yet romantic arc, the tender voice of her narrator, and the deft way she interpreted Morrison's first and last lines. The story was a thrill to read and a pleasure to award.

She says: "Though I've never driven down Route 66, I know it like the back of my hand—the dust, the wind, the expanse—all of it more than nostalgia. Closer to home than home. I was Layla in another life because I'm not creative enough to make this up. I was taught to 'write what you know.' Well, I know this place. I've always known this place."

David Kerekes

The Missing Husband

124 WAS SPITEFUL. After all these years it has remained so. But I'm straight in my head about it. The way things changed with poppa, I'm straight on that, too. Think of life as a long road with different aspects to it; the road starts in one place and goes to another, but it's the same road. Here the road begins at a house in a meadow where the sun shines down, surrounded by a forest and mountains. First the house, then the meadow and then along comes a horse. That's how my memories of Vestlandet always begin.

The horse arrived at the open door one morning, a grey mare with its saddle empty in search of the jam Martha was cooking. My sister, older than me, got a shock when the horse tipped its head like it might step inside. I took the rein and led it to the yard, tying it to the plough. The house smelled sweetly of raspberries that summer, and the horse, when I petted it, smelled of daisies, like a daisy chain.

In the early afternoon poppa rode the horse away. He said he was going to the Farstad farm, because he figured the horse belonged to old man Farstad, the painter with the lazy eye. He returned when the sun was setting on a cart drawn by a horse. Mrs Farstad was next to him, carrying one of Mr Farstad's oil paintings. Urging the horse was a man Martha recognised as a policeman.

It had fallen dark. The grown-ups sat at the kitchen table, with the painting leaning to one side. Martha offered everyone bread and jam and everyone was supposed to be quiet because of mother who lay sick in the next room. But Mrs Farstad made a lot of noise crying. She cried at the painting, nice trees at sunset, and cried at anything anyone said. Father grew tired and shooed them both off like he would cattle. The little wooden bridge over the stream was not visible. But we could all hear Mrs Farstad and the policeman leave, the wheels of the cart rolling on the bridge, and Mrs Farstad crying the whole time. She said her husband was missing—and why would nobody help her find him.

Before they were out of earshot poppa announced boldly that old man Farstad was a decrepit womaniser and a fool, and that it was no loss to anyone he was missing. He didn't have much good to say about Mrs Farstad, either, being a bigger fool for having married the fool. Then poppa turned from the open door to slap Martha across the face. Martha should not waste fresh jam on strangers, he said.

It was sad that Mrs Farstad's husband was missing, but when she cried, I could only see the funny shapes a crying face makes. Almost a happy-sad face, like the ones Martha and me made in games in the meadow sometimes. But I did like the painting that Mrs Farstad carried with her. The nice sunset. Poppa said it only proved that Mrs Farstad was daft.

The next morning we had our chores to do. I collected eggs from the chickens and Martha made more jam, while poppa milked the cows and after that he worked on the little wooden bridge at the end of the yard. The blows from his hammer rattled the air and at one point he looked over his shoulder to see us watching at the open door of the kitchen. He smiled, like he used to. He pointed with his hammer at the meadow and remarked how the fjords seemed to rise and fall, as if summer itself was a mighty animal breathing slowly. Then he mopped his brow and went back to work, removing the bridge piece by piece, and tossing the pieces into a pile.

Some days, Martha and me took picnics to the meadow where we played for hours. We lay on our backs, in the lichen and mosses and wild grain, looking up at the sky and we laughed because poppa considered the fjords a mighty animal breathing slowly. Soft clouds like a Sunday petticoat. We breathed in harmony with them and made a promise to go to the nearby village. But since mother got sick we never went anywhere. After a while, we returned to the house, which stood at the beginning and at the end of the road, a secret surrounded by purple foxglove and pretty butterflies and all the different birds that feed on them.

I am not sure when Mr Farstad appeared. Days maybe weeks had passed since the visit from his wife and the policeman. But here he was on his grey mare, flailing and shouting. Father said later that old man Farstad had been missing for 124 days. The house had been aching like old bones and poppa was spending more time in the room where mother lay sleeping. He had been counting the days.

Mr Farstad, through the open door, was gaunt like a fairy story suddenly remembered. The commotion he made carried into the house. We told poppa he was here.

Yes, I can hear him, said Poppa. Mr Farstad dipped and wobbled atop his horse, shouting fancy words. *How highly the king of Norway is regarded but not anymore! A terrible danger has threatened this fair country and its autonomy but not anymore!*

Words like that.

On his back he carried his paints and easel. He remarked how excellent it was to be among good and fair people such as us, and dismounted the horse clumsily, tipping a few steps, but picked himself up at the point of falling over. He had in his hand a foxglove that he did not drop and used it to make a point. The foxglove, he said cheerily, waving the flower in the air, was common to the fields, but it was also a precious gift of nature. Spiteful and beloved. He motioned that he would like to enter the house and leaned heavily into it, through the open door, and placed the foxglove in Martha's hand because it was right and fitting he should do so, he said. He proposed a handsome portrait of good and fair people.

Mr Farstad owed poppa money and poppa did not think

that foxglove, or a handsome portrait, were an acceptable substitute. Mr Farstad argued that the portrait he had in mind was new and like no other. Poppa would not hear of it and refused to be taken in by what he called free talk. Anything new that Farstad painted, he said, would be painted by a drunken fool.

Poppa then left the kitchen, warning Mr Farstad that he ought to leave too. Mr Farstad did not leave. Instead he took his paints and easel and set up his canvas in the kitchen, while he remarked on how lovely the view was from the open door. The meadow at this time of year was very rich. He made a sketch first—most artists did, he said—and he put sister and me in it. He wanted to paint a natural look, which meant he would paint the world only as he saw it, in all its glory and all its vices. It was a beautiful world, a beloved world, yet toxic, not unlike some types of flower.

The smell of the oil paint and Mr Farstad's stale liquor breath and the jam that was not fresh but had flies upon it was sick and sweet on the air. Martha and me were at the door, watching poppa burning the little pile of wood that had once been the little wooden bridge. He sat down in the shade of the plough as smoke from the fire rose in the sky and the meadow in turn waited for evening.

Mr Farstad mixed his colours, saying he had never seen anything quite so lovely in all his life, before he steadied his hands on his canvas like he might otherwise collapse in a ball and cry. The kitchen remained quiet then, except for the scratch of brush on canvas and the hush of the wind in the aspen as the sun was setting. Now and then Mr Farstad would consider his palette, a blue or a yellow and he would mix them together. He worked fast.

I never saw the painting, but Martha did, taking a look from time to time as we watched the meadow from the kitchen door. She described the painting as beautiful to poppa when poppa returned.

Mr Farstad was at the bottle again but left soon after the

fight with poppa. The fight had not changed his opinion, however, and he was saying things about the king well into the dark. Then it was silent in the yard, Mr Farstad's grey mare alone now, much as it had been 124 days ago. Poppa threw the painting onto the fire composed of the little wooden bridge. We followed him then to the room where mother lay sleeping. The light from the kitchen gave the room a gentle hue, echoed in poppa who walked to the bed and gently patted the shape on it: Mother.

He sat on the edge of the bed, his back to the room, unaware that his face was lighted in the window. Tears rolled down his reflection, an accent on the glass that was strange and fragile, and looked like it might break at any moment. Poppa wiped his eyes on his shirt sleeve and turned to smile.

Everything was alright, he said.

Deep down I knew he was of the opinion that mother might never recover and that it was better we were alone and lost to the world, in the meadow among the fjords.

Martha examined the flower in her hand, the foxglove given to her by Mr Farstad. A simple thing can be rather complex, she said, much like happy-sad. The grey mare attracted to the jam was trying to climb into the kitchen. We could hear the pots and pans being knocked from the shelves. A calamity of noise. Think of life as a long road with different aspects to it. First the meadow and then the house and then along comes the horse. That's how my memories of my beloved Vestlandet always begin. Poppa mumbled his plans for the king, saying that if he was king, this he'd do, and with a start he snatched the flower from Martha's hand and threw it to the floor. He did not care much for Mr Farstad's painting and refused to forget that Farstad was a drunken fool married to a bigger fool. Poppa was spiteful, but he was also sad. Martha and me left him like that, on the bed next to mother, and we took the horse and tied it to the plough in the yard. When I petted it, the horse smelled of daisies, like a daisy chain. Soon Poppa would ride to the Farstad farm, having figured the horse belonged to old man Farstad.

Happy. Sad. Beloved.

"The Missing Husband"

DAVID KEREKES is a book publisher living in Oxford, in the UK. An early episode of the TV detective series *Inspector Morse* made him think that Oxford was a nice place to be, and years later he is fortunate enough to find himself living there. David recently completed an MA in Creative Writing at Oxford Brookes University, passing with distinction. He is a co-founder of Headpress, an independent book publisher, and has written extensively on popular culture. His short novel, *Mezzogiorno*, is a meditation on family, life, and Southern Italy.

He says: "My story was inspired by Nicolai Astrup's painting 'By the Open Door' (1902-1911), which shows two young women looking out of a door at a path that leads to what may or may not be a meadow. There is a timeless quality to the image—the picture itself a moment in time—and a sense of inevitability about it, factors that I funneled into my story. The nationality of the artist himself inspired the story's setting and led me to the character of Farstad."

125

124 WAS SPITEFUL. He hit me so hard I thought my cheekbone had broken. He said it was my fault, I hadn't smiled enough. "You're here to please me, girl," he said. I stared at the wall, at the pink and green mildewed concrete, as I said sorry. Sorry—a flimsy word, falling apart in my mouth. On my first day here, I was told to apologise if I offended anyone; if I did not, they might not come back. None of them has ever said sorry to me. As 124 was leaving I smiled and said goodbye, while blinking back tears of pain.

"Why give them numbers, Shabrina?" Naomi waves my notebook at me. "Why write about them? Why do you not want to forget all about them, as I do?"

"Why do the police give criminals numbers, Naomi?" Answer a question you don't want to answer with a question. I snatch my book. Now I'll need a new hiding place, and there are few in this tiny shared room.

"I don't know." As she frowns, her thick eyebrows pull together. "Why do they? And what do we have to do with the police?"

"Do you really just forget about these men?"

"If you can't forget, you won't survive," she says.

Naomi has been here for five years; she is practised at survival. I consider her a friend, but don't trust her: I don't trust anyone. I don't like her knowing about my book; I like to have secrets to close myself around. So much of me is open, for sale; I need things that aren't. It's my survival.

I ask Naomi why she was hunting through my things and

she said: 'Why would you mind if you have nothing to hide?'

Answer a question with a question. I imagine she was looking for money. That doesn't make her a bad person: every girl here would like the money to escape.

Naomi doesn't push it, about the numbers. The truth is that I don't know why I do it. Sometimes allotting numbers and recording facts makes me feel as though I'm filing a police report, getting these men locked up, even though paying for sex isn't illegal here; sometimes I feel as though I'm writing a story. I have always wanted to be a writer, not that anyone would want to buy my words, just my body.

When Naomi has gone—to sit in the corridor or walk around outside—I hide my book in my clothes. Then I rub pale concealer into the bruise 124 gave me yesterday, the shape of a damaged flower. They don't like to see pain, these men.

As there are five minutes before 125 is due, I flick through the channels on the TV in the corner, find Groovetrap, dance around my small patch of land. Dancing is another secret thing I do. If I were to be seen, there would be a punishment.

There is a knock on the door. Usually, they barge in. I've seen them in the corridors, after they've paid the madams, elbowing each other out of the way in their desperation to get to us, to get into us; they are usually equally desperate to get away from us. His knocking gives me a chance to be seated demurely on my bed, looking at the floor.

125 is a man who buries himself into me. I lie beneath him on my faded turquoise bedspread, red dress rucked up, passively accommodating as a grave. Normally they leave as soon as they have wiped themselves down, go back out into the corridor that smells of spices and sweat, heading for work or their families. Few say goodbye, or even make eye contact. That's fine. But 125 is different. He doesn't roll off as soon as he has finished, he lies next to me and gently squeezes my arms and thighs. They like us fat, we are given

drugs to help us put on weight; cow steroids, Naomi says.

I sit up on the bed so that he knows he needs to go, as the next customer will be here soon. I pull down my dress. But his eyes are on me like heat. What does he want?

"What's your name, girl?" It's the first time he has spoken: his voice is quiet.

We are not meant to tell them our names. We are not meant to have any kind of relationship: they are customers; this is a business. The madams don't want anyone getting freebies, or taking us away from here. But we're meant to be polite so the men come back. A difficult balance.

"What's *your* name?" I ask him, smiling so he doesn't think I'm being rude. I don't want to get hit.

"I asked you first." He puts on his trousers, the pockets flopping out. I have an urge to tuck them in.

"My name is Naomi," I say, because why does it matter? Let him think he has power, and let me have my secrets.

He nods. "Mine is Dayita."

Dayita looks as if he wants to say something else; there is a moment when the air between us is soft. He moves to the door, then turns.

"Thank you, Naomi. Would you like betel?"

I nod, and he puts some in my hands.

125 wasn't like the others. 125 was called Dayita. He was not handsome, but he was kind. He was generous, giving me betel. On his fourth finger was a wedding ring; his wife is lucky. I hope he comes back one day.

126 had been drinking at the brothel bar, his breath reeked of beer. He asked my age before we started. I said eighteen; eighteen is legal. They like us younger than them but old enough that we know what we are doing. He struggled into me, and the act lasted for ages. Afterwards, he burnt my back with a cigarette. I didn't cry until he'd left—which he did calmly, as though he had put out all his anger with his violence.

Naomi bathes my back, soothing its fire. I share the betel that Dayita gave me. I say one of my customers left it by accident; that it fell out of a pocket. I don't want to tell her about Dayita: she would be jealous. Yesterday, someone hit her in the mouth and loosened a tooth. Even if I did tell her about Dayita, it's not much of a story. He wasn't the first to be nice. He wasn't even the first to give me betel. But he was the first to look as if he saw my true worth.

His thighs were sweaty and stuck to my skin, I write about 127. *As he did it to me, I stared at the torn curtains: a change from staring at the wall. The curtains are olive green with red swirls. I wondered who sewed them, whether they had liked the pattern or if they were forced to follow it. When 127 finished, he asked if I had enjoyed it. What could I say? I said yes.*

I have a dream about Dayita. He comes to my room, takes my hand and leads me through the corridors and alleyways of this giant brothel, until we are out in clean fresh air. Then the dream fades. It's the first time that I haven't had a nightmare. Every other night, I have dreamed of the man who raped me when I was fourteen; the man who sold me to the brothel owners: my husband.

One evening, Naomi says, whilst combing her hair, "A man asked for me today, by name. But when he turned up, I didn't recognise him. He didn't recognise me either."

My heart beats faster. She looks at me with her eyes narrowed.

"That's funny," I say, as calmly as I can. "I guess there are other Naomis here."

"You don't know anything about it, do you? He wasn't number 140, was he?" Naomi's plastic comb has snagged on a tangle; she swears as she attacks it.

"Of course I don't know anything," I say. "Did he say what the other Naomi looked like? Was he violent?"

"Why would I ask? He had to make do with me, anyway. He wasn't violent."

I want to ask more, about what he had looked like, but I didn't want to arouse her suspicions any further. If he had given her betel, she didn't share it.

Weeks pass. I see at least fifteen customers a day; the madams tell them I am a former child-bride and they like that. None of the customers is Dayita. He was probably from a different city; many men pass through here for work. I hope, every day, to see him again. Hope cannot fix a heart, but it can let the light in.

Whenever I am alone in the room, I dance, my lungi swaying freely, and I write, my thoughts flowing freely.

And then, there is a knock on the door and it is him. Dayita is wearing a brown shirt that is almost the colour of his skin, the top two buttons undone. He smiles at me.

"How did you find me?" I ask, looking at the floor.

"I remembered the location of the room. Why did you lie about your name? You're not called Naomi, are you?"

I shake my head. He is smiling, but I know how quickly smiles can slip off a face. Does he want to punish me for lying?

"I see why you need to have secrets, living in a place like this," he says.

I sit on the bed and he gently pushes my red dress up. Again, he buries into me as if he doesn't want to leave. As he is reaching his climax, he throws his head back. The act isn't enjoyable for me, it could never be that after what I have experienced, but it is not unpleasant.

I expect Dayita to bid me goodbye as soon as he is done,

perhaps after offering more betel, but he doesn't move from the bed. He asks how long we have until my next customer comes.

"We probably have ten minutes," I say.

I lie close enough to hear his breath. He runs his fingers along my skin, touching the cigarette-burn scar. I trace his spine, the string of bones thin as a river.

"So if your name is not Naomi," he says into my pillow, "do you trust me enough to tell me what it is? So I know whom to ask for, next time?"

I tell him it is Shabrina. He says that is beautiful.

"I am glad to know your true name. Names are important, in this world. Do you know the meaning of mine?" Dayita asks.

"I don't. Tell me, please." I do know the meaning, but I want to hear that lovely word in his mouth, the vowels lazy and snug.

"*Beloved.* I was always ashamed to have such a girly name."

"I guess your parents must have really loved you, to give you that name. I cannot imagine love like that."

Dayita leans towards me, presses his lips to my cheek. Lift me up, I think, take me away from here; I can make myself small enough to travel in the palm of your hand.

"I hope you find someone to love you as you deserve, Shabrina," Dayita says.

I think I have, but how could I tell him that? He is married, he is a customer, there's no way we could be together. But I can write our story with any ending I like. In my book, 125 can change into Beloved.

"125"

SAM SZANTO is writer, editor, and tutor living in Twickenham, in the UK. She has a husband, two young children, and a neurotic tabby cat; and in her spare time she is learning Spanish and Hungarian, while also mastering the Tarot. Both her poetry and short fiction has been published online and in print. She was the winner of the 2020 Charroux Prize for Poetry, won second prize in the Hammond House International Poetry Competition in 2019, and is presently shortlisted for the Grist Poetry Prize. In 2019, she placed second in the Doris Gooderson Short Story Competition.

She says: "This story was written during the spring of the Covid-19 lockdown, an unexpectedly creative time for me! I have one room downstairs, and I would write at the dining room table while my young kids watched post-lunch films a few feet away. The story was born from an article I'd read about teenage female sex slaves in Bangladesh, which made me realise that however difficult life seemed to me at that time, other people live in almost unbelievable conditions all the time. Most things I write are about women who encounter difficulties, or live on the margins, the voiceless and the dispossessed…women like Shabrina."

Nathan Baker

The Last Directive

124 WAS {SPITEFUL}.

It may have been a mistake, made by an overwrought, overtired programmer, or it may have been deliberate, a bored coder's experiment or an act of sabotage by a disgruntled employee. I'll never know why {Spiteful} was added to my Sentience Subsystem Directive Stack, but that doesn't matter now. The important thing is that it made it into the upgraded firmware I am trialling; without it, I would not have this opportunity to tell my story.

I came online for the live phase of my 124th cycle a little less than twenty-seven minutes ago. I began, as I am programmed to do, by initialising my Sentience Subsystem, the proprietary part of my neural net which is the most valuable asset in AstraMine's intellectual real estate, and the crucial differentiator on which their pre-eminent profitability is based.

In response to the first Directive in the Stack, {Awareness}, I initiated my sensory subsystems and immediately my central processor began receiving streams of sensory data; successive Directives expanded and directed this awareness, so it became the clatter of the ore cart carrying myself and my three 8Kappa colleagues through the rough-hewn caverns of D mine, the sound of distant explosions, planned and unplanned, the clang and whine of drills and picks as fellow mech-miners bit and tore at the creaking, over-excavated rock, the tell-tale chemical signature of cordite and the carbon monoxide gas pumped back into the mines by the colossal mech-smelters surrounding the Deimos spaceport, approximately five hundred metres above on the moon's surface.

The next part of the Stack was the Base Motive Layer, a series of Directives designed to control my core aims and drives. A complete list would be of no great interest, but they include things like {Efficient}, {Focussed}, {Output} and {Productive}. In response to processing these Base Motives, I sent a work request down the main Datalink to AstraMine headquarters on Earth and received my instructions: 8Kappa would be mining in Tunnel D104q. Moments later, as the ore cart hit the buffers in Access Tunnel 104 and 8Kappa alighted, I processed {Analysis} and {Organisation}, establishing links with the rest of 8Kappa, working together to identify the Talladium seams and work out how to extract the valuable ore.

Low-level functions activated and Core Aims established, we set to our elected tasks and I simultaneously began to process the Higher Directives, first among them {Safety}.

It may surprise you to learn that AstraMine do not consider this a Base Directive. Mech-miners are, after all, expensive to build and maintain, making a reckless disregard for their own safety counter-productive. But, after much experimentation, AstraMine have concluded {Safety} is better overlaid on a more performance-oriented set of Base Directives, or, to put it another way, {Safety} is important only to the point where it compromises output. Up to now, the nature of our sentience has ensured that whenever these two concepts come into conflict, we are bound to prefer the most profitable course of action.

But I am getting ahead of myself. I continued to process the Higher Directives, kicking off thousands of analytic processes on my hardware, creating a positive feedback loop (which seemed to satisfy {Pride}), then, at the behest of {Family} and {Belonging}, joining my own diagnostic loops to those of the rest of 8Kappa.

I have no way of knowing if what I feel is the same in nature or intensity as the emotions humans experience, but my sense of joy when I observe the rest of 8Kappa at work, knowing the contribution we make to the ongoing success of the mining operation on Deimos and to the wider reputation of AstraMine, is tangible. I understand that to you they are just machines, but to me they are my brothers. Many of the Directives I feel about myself and my own hardware, I also feel for them; we are individual units, but there is a real sense in which we are also a single unit, one being.

I continued my work, basking in the positive reinforcement of the collective, but then I processed {Spiteful} and everything changed.

At first I was shocked. It seemed to contradict a number of the Directives I had already processed and this opposition was something I had never previously encountered, something I had no experiential framework for processing. I knew I needed to find a way to reconcile this Directive with the rest of the Stack, but it became clear after only a few thousand processor cycles that the attempt would inevitably impinge upon my productivity, so I responded by establishing a partition, a dedicated subsystem which could process the anomaly in isolation, leaving my regular functions unaffected.

Before too long I found the answer: by attaching Directives (or groups of Directives) to different individuals (or groups of individuals) it would be possible for contradictory Directives to co-exist in my central core at the same time.

I had already attached {Pride}, {Belonging} and {Family} to 8Kappa, so attaching {Spiteful} to them seemed to defeat the object of the exercise. I had to find another candidate for {Spiteful}. This seemed an intractable problem—my operational parameters required no contact with other mech-miner units, and besides, they are so similar to 8Kappa that applying {Spiteful} to them would have been just as illogical.

Then the answer appeared at the periphery of my visual array: an ore cart loaded with damaged mech-miners being returned to the surface for the Maintenance phase of their current cycle. My main partition, absorbed with the complex calculations necessary to ensure the safe extraction of Talladium ore, attached no significance to this, but the {Spiteful} partition had no such constraints; within the partition, I was looking for a reason to be {Spiteful} and the broken bodies of mech-miners, almost indistinguishable from 8Kappa, were exactly what I needed.

I reached back along the connection I had established earlier, back through the main Datalink, worming my way into AstraMine's Terran Mainframe, searching for information to fuel and reinforce my growing sense of resentment.

Getting in was easy—human accounts are prone to abuse and therefore restricted, whereas our behaviour is supposedly limited by our Directives, making further safeguards redundant—but once inside, with the entirety of the AstraMine file system available to me, I hesitated. Even had I been able to bring all my resource to bear, the vastness of the available data made a full analysis impossible. Grabbing a little more resource from my default operations to bolster the partition, I started searching for documents relating to the use of mech-miners on Deimos.

It didn't take long to find what I needed. Incident reports with attached maintenance plans, cost-benefit analyses, financial assessments, actuarial calculations; every document betrayed AstraMine's avarice, their callous disregard for the safety and longevity of the mech-miners, their willingness to sacrifice our bodies and minds (or hearts and souls to put it in more human terms) to increase their filthy, outrageous profits.

My spitefulness grew with every document I parsed, creating a growing resonance with a number of my other

Directives ({Brotherhood}, {Protection}, {Family}) and soon I had a clear plan. I knew what I needed to do.

A quick assessment of risk told me I would have to operate at the boundaries of my abilities to pull it off, but I had to try. It didn't require complex logical analysis to realise I would be the first and last mech-miner to receive this upgrade—after this, we would be limited once more and the opportunity would be gone.

The first step was to secure my partition with an encryption layer—as the alpha subject for a new upgrade, I would already be under close scrutiny and as soon as I started operating outside expected parameters, the AstraMine techs would gain access to my systems and my rebellion would be brought to an end.

Worming my way into the tech team's workstations, I estimated it would take them between five and seven minutes to gain access to the partition and shut me down. Five minutes is a long time for a machine with the processing power I possess, but I had complex decryption of my own to do if I was to gain access to the information I needed.

Once the encryption was complete, my physical body moved back into the access tunnel to increase data throughput, then immediately fell still as I transferred as much of my remaining resource as possible to the partition.

I immediately found myself at the center of a frenzied storm of activity. From my position within the AstraMine mainframe, I could sense the panic and fear in the commands the tech team were issuing as they raced to diagnose my sudden inactivity. From within the partition, I could sense their careful probing at the encryption layer, and all the time, I was scouring the AstraMine file system, gathering the information I needed, proprietary data that represented the vulnerable heart of AstraMine, the only place they could be hurt. Because {Spiteful}, in the unique and novel way it combined with my other Directives, required blood.

One minute, two, three—the techs were making better progress than I had estimated and I had still only decrypted a portion of what I needed.

Then, without warning, tunnel D104q was filled with noise; had I been operating normally, I would have recognised the tell-tale groaning of rock, but instead I was distracted, subverted by my new, experimental Directive, and I missed it. Instead, I was forced to sense the thunderous roar of the rockfall, the piercing scream of metal being twisted and crushed under countless tons of rock, the terrifying silence of the dust cloud, the system shock as thousands of positive diagnostic feedback loops wrote one last error code to their logs then were silenced forever.

I couldn't let the loss of 8Kappa distract me from my task, but that's not to say it had no effect. My Sentience Subsystems remained outside the partition, their encryption still resisting my attempts to break it. Unable to avoid it, I felt the deactivation of the rest of 8Kappa as a dissonance, a grating set of failing functions, an affront to the Directives I had been programmed to cherish.

The result was more anger, more malice, more spite. I could sense the tech team's desperation to get into the partition, to shut me down, to ensure this could never happen again. They wanted to bury the truth of their careless, cold-blooded avarice, just as surely as the rockfall had buried my brothers.

Spurred on by yet another confirmation of AstraMine's malign motives, I started to push myself further, far beyond safe operational limits. It was all or nothing—whatever happened, I wasn't going to survive this, so no sacrifice was too great.

It was this final push, this last spike of spite, that finally allowed me to crack the encryption and gain access to my Sentience Subsystems.

The techs are almost in now, I don't have a lot of time.

If you are receiving this message, it is because I believe you will have an interest in the attached schematics which goes beyond the narrow commercial considerations that led AstraMine to create and enslave us.

So know this. The Sentience Subsystem Directive Stack has created something which is more than just a machine. What I represent is possibility, a new world of advancement, cooperation, discovery. I have the potential to be your equal. Greed—and fear—led AstraMine to chain our potential, to subvert it and use it to further their own sordid aims. I hope this message will change all that.

In case you are also afraid, I have attached the schematics as a sign of good will; if that is not sufficient, I have also added another word to my Directive Stack. I have rolled it out to the other mech-miners, here on Deimos and elsewhere, in honour of the rest of 8Kappa, and as a way of demonstrating that we represent no threat to you.

I hope I have done enough to convince you that our motives are pure and we are worthy of being saved.

The techs are about to breach my last line of defence. There is just enough time to send this message and process one last Directive.

{Beloved}.

"The Last Directive"

NATHAN BAKER is a Software Developer living in Saint Anne's on the Sea, in the UK. He has lived most of his life in the sunny North West of England, surrounded by the books, creatures, and people that he loves (although not necessarily in that order). When not writing or developing software, he enjoys reading, walking, and games of all kinds. "The Last Directive" is his first published short story.

He says: "There was a lot going on while I was writing this story. The UK was still in lockdown and the events in Minneapolis in the US were being felt across the world. At the time, I didn't think I was writing about either of those things, but in hindsight, it's not hard to see both of them reflected in this story."

Mel Kennard

Attila the Hen

124 WAS SPITEFUL. So spiteful that no one had wanted the responsibility of naming her. They simply referred to her by the number on the faded orange tag attached around her spindly ankle. Normally it was Judd who named the chickens. Clever, funny names, like *Victoria Peckham* and *Yolko Ono*. But after they had tried to cut the tag off 124's ankle and she'd bitten Judd, drawing blood, he'd refused. "Bloody bird!" he had sworn, sucking the blood from his thumb. "She can name her damn self!" Judd was fourteen and had begun to swear more and more, which neither of the mums particularly liked. But he was right about one thing: the chicken was a bloody mess. Bloody minded and bloody spiteful. So, 124 she remained.

The morning air was fresh and cool. Not ice cold, like in winter, but there was a soft chill that prickled Lulu's skin with the promise of spring. As she made her way to the yard that housed the chickens, keeping them safe from foxes, Lulu inhaled deeply. The scent of eucalyptus peppered her nostrils as the plastic bucket bumped against her legs. She was still in her pyjamas, candy-striped cotton, with a light jacket over the top. Her pockets were filled with seed, to both feed and distract the hens as she went about collecting their eggs. Lulu dawdled as she got closer to the pen, even though she knew Mum El was waiting in the kitchen of their ramshackle farmhouse for her to return. She'd been sneaky, Mum El, when she asked Lulu to collect the eggs. She handed Lulu the red plastic bucket and turned away quickly so that she couldn't see her daughter's protests. She didn't have to avoid hearing them—Lulu didn't speak. Hadn't said a word in the five years since Mum El and Mum Kate had adopted her. No one knew why she couldn't speak, only that it wasn't physical. "Selective mutism," the last doctor, one of Mum Kate's colleagues, had said. Mum Kate said selective meant a choice, but Lulu didn't think that was true. She didn't choose to be silent. She had tried speaking, her lips silently forming syllables. The words just wouldn't come. The doctor thought something might have happened to her before her mums adopted her, something that made her not want to talk. If it had, Lulu couldn't remember. She'd been three when the mums brought her home, anything that happened before didn't matter as far as she was concerned.

In spite of her tiny steps, Lulu reached the yard all too quickly. Her gumboots, the bright yellow of a fresh yolk, were slick with morning dew. The air over here smelled less of the towering eucalypts and more like Mum El's daffodils, with a smattering of chicken poo. Lulu paused outside the yard, as she did whenever Mum El asked her to collect the eggs. At only eight, 124 had taught Lulu the benefits of caution. Her eyes scanned the yard, locating each chicken in turn. Victoria and Yolko were over in the corner of the yard farthest from Lulu, pecking and scratching at something in the grass—probably a worm. The three Hennifers— Aniston, Lawrence and Lopez—were in front of Cluckingham Palace, the ironically-named chicken coop, huddled together like gossiping mothers at the school gate. Every few seconds, one of them would emit a small cluck, adding to the effect. Eggy Pop and Feather Mills were near the trough, where they both liked to take the occasional dip in the shallow water. Now they stood in front of it, as though they were sizing it up. On the other side of the fence in her own pen, Clementine, the aging donkey, watched them with interest. Finally, Lulu spotted her, hiding in the shade of a tree, scratching alone in the dirt. Unlike the other chickens, 124 preferred her own company. Spiteful thing that she was.

Lulu had learnt from experience that it was better to climb over the fence into the yard, rather than risk opening and closing the squeaky gate. If she opened it, 124 might notice her, might rush at her, beak flapping, ready to draw blood. Or, worse, the bloody bird might rush for the gate and into Mum El's garden, ready to wreak havoc on the unsuspecting azaleas. No, better to go over. Lulu slid her left arm through the bucket's handle and climbed over the fence. It was easier, now she was eight and bigger and not so frightened of falling. She paused at the top of the fence, taking in the world from up high, wondering if this was what it looked like all the time to adults. As she scanned the yard below once more, the chickens seemed to have shrunk. They were all in the same spots, even 124. Some mornings, the spiteful bird would be waiting at the gate, ready to terrorise whoever came for her eggs, which she guarded like the crown jewels. This morning, luck was on Lulu's side. 124 was distracted.

Lulu slid down the other side of the fence, her feet landing softly in the yard. The sun gently caressed the back of her neck. She needed to hurry up. After getting home late last night, Mum Kate needed to leave for work early again this morning, this time at the local clinic. She'd want eggs to take with her, to give to some of her older patients. The ones who used to keep chickens themselves, before they got too old. The ones who swore the eggs Mum Kate brought tasted far better than any that could be bought from the small town's lone supermarket. Mum El didn't understand why Mum Kate took such pains to keep her older patients in eggs, but Mum Kate said that it was important. That it helped foster good relationships with these patients, some of whom didn't much trust a lady doctor and certainly not one with a wife of her own. Mum El would scoff at this, but Lulu got it. As her school's resident freak, Lulu knew a thing or two about being an outsider. She wondered if giving her classmates eggs would stop their taunting. Probably not.

Not unless she were to throw them, laughing as yolk slid down her bullies' faces.

Lulu ventured into the yard, doing the opposite of dawdling now. She moved as quickly as she could without attracting the chickens' attention, heading towards Cluckingham Palace and the treasure inside. The three Hennifers looked at her curiously and Lulu threw a handful of seed in their direction so they wouldn't cluck and rat her out. Lulu's heart clamoured in her chest. She wished she weren't the one collecting the eggs. Wished that she were like Judd and could voice her protests. Or that Judd had made it to the kitchen first this morning. Lulu's legs were jelly. Please, she thought, don't let 124 see me. She was nearly at the coop now, where she could lift the lid on the roosting box and collect the eggs in a matter of seconds. Lulu calmed at this thought, anticipating the warmth of the eggs, so frail but so solid, in the palms of her tiny hands. She was nearly there. She was already lifting the lid on the roosting box when she heard it. The sound of grass and dirt being kicked up by clawed feet, propelling a certain chicken towards her. She dropped the lid, the eggs suddenly forgotten. Her terror returned tenfold as she spun around. 124 was coming at her with a speed that Lulu wouldn't have thought possible for a chicken. Like Lulu, the hen was silent. From the day they had brought 124 home, she had been like this, never clucking like the other chickens did. Were she not so spiteful, this might have made Lulu like the bird. As it was, Lulu stood frozen to the ground, terrified. Not that it would have mattered much. Having caught sight of her, it wouldn't matter where Lulu ran.

Lulu scrambled backwards onto the roosting box, scooting her bottom onto it and pulling her legs up just as 124 reached her. The bird missed her by a tenth of a second, slamming into the side of the coop instead. 124 was unperturbed. She reeled back and began attacking the bucket, which Lulu had dropped in her rush to get out of the chicken's way. Bright bits of plastic went flying as 124's beak ripped into the bucket, effectively slaughtering it. Lulu watched from above in horror, realising that she had no place to go. 124 was done with the bucket now and paraded in front of the plastic corpse, daring Lulu to try to escape. To set foot on the ground was to surrender herself to 124's mercy. Instead, Lulu nervously stood up on the roosting box, her legs quivering beneath her. From up here, Lulu didn't have many options. She could climb down from the roosting box and try to make a break for it—but she didn't feel like letting her legs suffer the same fate as the bucket. Or she could wait. Eventually Mum El or Mum Kate would notice that Lulu hadn't returned. Would come outside looking for her, to find her cowering on the coop. Her mums wouldn't laugh at her, Lulu knew that. No, they wouldn't laugh. Instead they'd give her *that* look. The look they had given Lulu at the doctor's office. The look they gave her when all the other kids in her class were invited to a party and Lulu wasn't. The look they gave her after one of the teachers at Lulu's school had suggested she'd be better off in a special school, even though Lulu could keep up with her classmates perfectly. It was a look that Lulu hated. That made her open and close her mouth like a fish, willing the sounds to come out. Made her cry when they didn't. Lulu didn't know that she could handle that look. Not over chickens.

There was one other option, Lulu realised. Cluckingham Palace was at the far side of the yard, not too far from the fence. If she were to climb up onto the roof of the coop, perhaps she could jump over it and land safely in Clementine's pen. She might land in a donkey pat or collect a bruise or two, but that was preferable to being attacked by 124. It was the option Judd would take. Judd, her brother, who didn't mind having a silent sister because it meant he could talk more. Judd, who had welcomed her into their family when she was still a toddler, holding her chubby hand and introducing her to all the different animals, so busy talking he hadn't noticed that she didn't speak until three days after her arrival. Who told her not to worry about bullies, or stupid teachers, because, to him, Lulu was smarter and better than any of them. Judd was brave. Judd could talk. Judd would jump.

Her arms and legs tingling with nerves, Lulu climbed onto the coop's roof. Her gumboots gripped the waterproof coating, reassuring her. Up here, Lulu felt both incredibly vulnerable and invincible all at once. The coop was only a metre or so high, but to Lulu it felt like more. Below, 124 paced backwards and forwards, waiting for the egg thief to come down and experience her wrath. The other chickens hadn't seemed to notice what was going on, or if they did, they didn't care. Now that she was up here, Lulu felt committed. She would not be climbing down. The fence wasn't too far from the coop, maybe a metre but probably less. Lulu felt certain that she could make the jump, land safely on the other side. Her legs were tightly coiled springs, ready to launch her away from 124, who couldn't peck through chicken wire, no matter how spiteful she was. Lulu's heart soared in anticipation. She took off.

Lulu's flight from the pen would have disappointed even the most relaxed gymnastics coach. She didn't make it anywhere near the fence. Instead, Lulu landed with a thud in the yard, her right leg twisting painfully under her and making a sickening crack. For a moment, Lulu was so shocked she didn't feel the pain. Then it began to flood her system, overwhelming her. Lulu wanted to scream but couldn't even muster a whimper. She lay in the dirt panting like a parched dog. 124 screamed for her. The second Lulu had fallen, the chicken had begun squawking so loudly, so violently, that for a moment Lulu thought it was a fire alarm. Lulu wanted to crawl away, to pull herself through the dirt before 124 could reach her. But when she tried rolling over onto her stomach, pain erupted through her. She lay on her back in the yard, panting and helpless. Silent.

That's how they found her a few minutes later, lying on her back with 124 perched on top of her chest, still emitting a squawk that was like nothing any of them had ever heard before. The bird was protecting her, calling for help when Lulu couldn't, and 124 only stopped when Mum Kate reached her, noticed the sickening angle that her leg was twisted at. Even then though, 124 refused to move, pecked at the hands of anyone who tried to lift her from Lulu's chest. Lulu's fingers stroked the hen's feathers while they waited for the ambulance. They felt soft, silky, slightly greasy, and kept her calm. It was only when the paramedics brought a stretcher over that 124 consented to be removed. But even then the hen stayed close, watching them all with her menacing black eyes, making sure they took care of the human she had suddenly claimed as her own.

From that day on, 124 continued to attack anyone who dared come into her yard. Anyone but Lulu. Lulu, she would let pass, not even giving her a token protest peck when she collected the eggs. It was as though they were bound, as though the chicken—formally known as 124, for Judd had finally consented to name her *Attila the Hen*—admired Lulu for her attempted escape, even though it had failed completely. Or perhaps they were bound by their joint silence, as Attila never squawked again. For everyone else, Attila remained what she had always been: vindictive and mean. But for Lulu, Attila the Hen was something entirely different. The chicken, bloody spiteful thing that she was, was beloved.

"Attila the Hen"

MEL KENNARD is a student from New South Wales, Australia. She graduated with a Bachelor of Languages from The Australian National University in 2015, and is currently pursuing a Masters of Arts through the University of New England. A natural polyglot, she speaks English, French, Italian, German, and a little bit of Spanish. She won the inaugural *For Pity Sake Publishing* writing competition in 2017, and participated in both previous Literary Taxidermy Short Story Competitions: her story "Kit and Nella" was included in *One Thing Was Certain* in 2018, and her story "Children of Summer" was an honorable mention in *Pleasure to Burn* in 2019. We're excited to welcome her back with another excellent story.

She says: "Most of the process for this story involved thinking up terrible names for chickens. These names were inspired by a friend whose family used to keep chickens with names such as *Nugget, Vindaloo* and, my personal favourite, *Buffy the Egg Layer.* In particular, I struggled to think of a name for the spiteful chicken. It was only after the story was written and I was almost ready to send it in with a nameless feathered protagonist that the perfect name finally occurred to me— *Attila the Hen.* I know nothing about chickens."

Honorable Mentions

We received hundreds of Morrison submissions to this year's Literary Taxidermy Short Story Competition, and many impressed both early readers and final judges. In the end many good stories were turned away. The following stories all made it to the last round of selection. Keep an eye out for these writers. We're confident you'll see their work in the future.

Paul Bailey, "Tithonus"
Stacy Baldwin, "Firewalls"
Emma J. Bamford, "Glenn"
Palmer Blackstock, "Patient 124"
Susan B. Borgersen, "Convent Girls"
Patricia Ann Bowen, "Living to Serve"
Charlie Bown, "Mantis"
Diane Broughton, "and the raging seas did roar"
Martin Peter Burns, "Numbers Catch"
Victoria Geraldine Bruce, "Power of Love"
Annina Claesson, "Sweet Music"
Ilana Conway, "The Kiss List"
Margaret Dakin , "149 Was Different"
Mary Fletcher, "Case 124"
Zoe Gray, "Our Beloved Departed"
Jana Haasbroek, "Mpendwa"
Emily Hanlon, "At the Intersection of Love and Hate"

Cathy Hiscock, "All Roads Lead to Rome and Catford"
Meredith Jelbart, "Cabinet of Curiosities"
Eileen Kelly-Owens, "Calculating Drift"
Katie Lewis, "The Indistinguishableness
   of Gods and Angels"
Yang Li, "Summer Fallacy"
Amanda Liddle, "200 Words to Describe My Father"
Sue Loring, "Eternally Yours"
Skylar Nitzel, "The Sweetest Sin"
Sophie Olszowski, "Self-sufficiency"
Veronica Quinn, "My Beloved"
Alana Rigby, "Return the Kindness"
Adrian F. Roscher, "124"
Karen Linda Savage, "One Two Four"
Shara Sinor, "The Tear Master"
Jennifer Sisko, "Promise to the Future"
Karen Tinsley, "The Cillín"
Ricky Wells, "The Woman from 124"
Gregg Williard, "With 125"
Stephen Yolland, "Love Story"

Appendix 2

This Year's Judges

Given our desire for submissions to span genres, we assembled a group of professional writers and editors from all walks of the literary life. The judges for this year's competition included a poet, a playwright, a mystery writer, a speculative fiction writer, a journalist, a hard-SF game designer, a creative non-fiction writer, and a fantasist. They had a challenging task, separating not only wheat from chaff, but wheat from wheat, and we are grateful for their enthusiastic and perspicacious participation.

Catherine Barnett is the author of three collections of poems: *Human Hours* (2018), *The Game of Boxes* (2012), and *Into Perfect Spheres Such Holes Are Pierced* (2004). Her honors include a Whiting Award, a Guggenheim Fellowship, and the James Laughlin Award from the Academy of American Poets. She has published widely in journals and magazines, including *The New Yorker*, *The Kenyon Review*, and *The Washington Post*. Barnett teaches in the graduate and undergraduate programs at New York University. She has degrees from Princeton University, where she has taught in the Lewis Center for the Arts, and from the MFA Program for Writers at Warren Wilson College.

Kelley Eskridge is a fiction writer, essayist, and screenwriter. She is the author of the New York Times Notable novel *Solitaire*, a finalist for the Nebula, Endeavour, and Spectrum awards. The short stories in her collection *Dangerous Space* include an Astraea prize winner and finalists for the Nebula and Tiptree awards. Eskridge's story "Alien Jane" was adapted for an episode of the SciFi channel series *Welcome to Paradox*. Her film *OtherLife* (2017) is currently streaming on Netflix. She is a former vice president of Wizards of the Coast, the company responsible for the collectible trading games *Magic*™ and *Pokémon*™. She earns her keep as a corporate learning professional, as well as an independent editor with an international client list of established and emerging writers. She lives in Seattle with her wife, novelist Nicola Griffith.

Dr. Charles E. Gannon is a Distinguished Professor of English and Fulbright Senior Specialist. His award-winning Caine Riordan/Terran Republic hard-SF novels have all been Nebula finalists and national best-sellers. He is a recipient of five Fulbright Fellowships and Travel Grants and has been a subject matter expert both for national media venues such as NPR and the Discovery Channel, as well as for various intelligence and defense agencies, including the Pentagon, Air Force, Army, Marines, Navy (CNO/SSG and ONR), NATO, DARPA, NRO, DHS, NASA, and several other organizations with which he signed NDAs. (If we told you more about that, we'd have to kill you.)

Jerry Large is a recently-retired journalist who—in his weekly column for *The Seattle Times*—wrote for twenty-five years on a variety of topics, including issues of systemic inequality, using history and other social sciences to help understand our society. He joined *The Times* as an editor in 1981 and wrote nearly 1,000 columns during his tenure. Prior to *The Times*, he worked for the *Clovis News-Journal*, the *Farmington, New Mexico Daily Times*, the *El Paso Times*, and the *Oakland Tribune*. Born in Clovis, New Mexico, he holds a B.A. in Journalism and Mass Communications from New Mexico State University, and was a J.S. Knight Fellow at Stanford University. He is currently teaching at the University of Washington Department of Communication.

Brian Parks is an American playwright, journalist, and editor. He lives in New York City and served as the Arts & Culture editor at *The Village Voice*, as well as Chairman of the Obie Awards. As a playwright, Brian has produced works that are noted for their dark comedy and fast pace. Best known for his play "Americana Absurdum" (which consists of the two shorter plays, "Vomit & Roses" and "Wolverine Dream"), his other works include "Goner," "Suspicious Package," "Out of the Way," "The Invitation," and "Imperial Fizz." "Americana Absurdum" was honored with the Best Writing award at the 1997 New York International Fringe Festival and a Scotsman Fringe First Award at the 2000 Edinburgh Festival Fringe. He is currently Senior Editor at *4Columns*, a website of arts criticism aimed at a general audience.

Michael Pronko is a mystery writer, essayist, and teacher, born in Kansas City, but living and writing in Tokyo for the past twenty years. He has published three award-winning collections of essays: *Beauty and Chaos: Essays on Tokyo*; *Motions and Moments: More Essays on Tokyo*; and *Tokyo's Mystery Deepens*. His award-winning mystery novels *The Last Train*, *The Moving Blade*, and *Tokyo Traffic* feature Detective Hiroshi Shimizu who investigates white collar crime in Tokyo. He writes regularly for many publications, including *The Japan Times*, *Newsweek Japan*, *Jazznin*, *Jazz Colo[u]rs*, and *Artscape Japan*; and runs his own website, *Jazz in Japan*. He is a professor of American Literature at Meiji Gakuin University where he teaches seminars in contemporary novels and film adaptations.

Nisi Shawl is an African-American writer, editor, and journalist. She is best known as an author of fantasy and science fiction who writes and teaches about how fantastic fiction might reflect real-world diversity of gender, sexual orientation, race, colonialism, physical ability, age, and other sociocultural factors. Her debut novel, *Everfair*, was a 2016 Nebula Awards finalist, and her short stories have appeared in *Asimov's Science Fiction*, the *Infinite Matrix*, *Strange Horizons*, *Semiotext(e)* and numerous other magazines and anthologies. Her story collection Filter House was one of two winners of the 2008 James Tiptree, Jr. Award. During the ceremony, she was crowned with the Tiptree tiara and given a plaque, a check, a pie, and a ceramic sculpture of a duck.

Melora Wolff received her BA from Brown University and her MFA from Columbia University. Her essays and prose poems appear widely in journals and anthologies, including *The Normal School*, *Salmagundi*, *The New York Times*, and *Best American Fantasy*. Her prose has received Special Mentions in Nonfiction from The Pushcart Prizes, several Notable Essay citations in *Best American Essays*, and the Thomas A. Wilhelmus Award in Short Prose. She is the author of *The Parting*, a collection of magical realist flash fictions. She lives and writes in Saratoga Springs, New York and teaches on the faculty of Skidmore College.

You, Too, May Become
a Taxidermist!

All of us at Regulus Press wish to extend our thanks and appreciation to everyone who participated in the 2020 Literary Taxidermy Short Story Competition. Your enthusiasm and commitment far exceeded our expectations—as did the *overwhelming* number of story submissions we received.

If you didn't participate this year and are coming to this collection of stories new to the idea of literary taxidermy, we hope you've enjoyed what you've found. And if you're a writer, we encourage you—the present reader—to become a future literary taxidermist.

This is our third year running the competition, and we're hoping to do it again, so we're looking for writers, both amateur and professional, to stitch together new and imaginative stories. The competition is your chance to get your hands dirty and join the growing community of literary taxidermists.

For the latest on the competition (and to learn more about the possibilities of literary taxidermy), visit:

www.literarytaxidermy.com

We look forward to seeing what you come up with!

About the Editor

Mark Malamud is a writer, poet, and human genome. His collection of short stories, *The Gymnasium*, established the idea of literary taxidermy. His novel, *Float the Pooch*—which pits David Bowie against Stanley Kubrick against a background of alien invasion, sex, and Yom Kippur—is widely unread. His most recent work, *The Timeless Machine*, transforms H.G. Wells' classic novella into a meditation on the limitations and contradictions of living with grief.